Lucifer and Lacious

Lucifer and Lacious

by
Sean Vincent Lehosit

DORRANCE PUBLISHING CO., INC.
PITTSBURGH, PENNSYLVANIA 15222

This is a work of fiction. Names, characters, places, and incidents are either the product of the author's imagination or are used fictitiously, and any resemblance to actual persons, living or dead; events; or locales is entirely coincidental.

All Rights Reserved
Copyright © 2007 by Sean Vincent Lehosit
No part of this book may be reproduced or transmitted in any form or by any means, electronic or mechanical, including photocopying, recording, or by any information storage and retrieval system without permission in writing from the publisher.

ISBN: 978-0-8059-7270-2
Library of Congress Control Number: 2006924659
Printed in the United States of America

First Printing

For more information or to order additional books, please contact:
Dorrance Publishing Co., Inc.
701 Smithfield Street
Third Floor
Pittsburgh, Pennsylvania 15222
U.S.A.
1-800-788-7654
www.dorrancebookstore.com

Acknowledgment

I would like to thank my mother and family for their support for my love of writing. Without her support this story may not have been possible.

Prologue

I had awoken as saliva ran down my chin and spilled onto my air mattress, which formed a small puddle beneath my cheek. The room felt so cold against my skin; the thin blanket spread across my naked body did very little to keep me warm. Frozen vapors expelled from my cracked dry lips, so with each heaving breath I stumbled to the beat of my shaking bones.

I had no idea where I was or why I was there. What was most disturbing to me though was that I could not remember my name. Not for the life of me. Scanning the room I managed to find myself an old pair of gray Ohio State sweatpants, a wrinkled old tank top smelling of baked ham, and a damp pair of boots tucked away in the corner of the small dimly lit room.

Peering down the staircase, I descended toward the lower level of the house not knowing what or who I may find. I parted a purple tattered sheet that segregated the stairway from the living space and entered the next room. For a brief second I felt a warm breeze blow against my shivering body, but it quickly faded once more into bitter coldness.

The house seemed to be empty. It felt antiqued and abandoned; the type of house a dead man might live in. I began to explore the house, first I entered the kitchen. The kitchen smelled of moldy bread and spoiled milk. Crumbs of previous meals laid scattered amongst the countertops. Crushed cans of vegetables littered the ground, which I kicked as I shuffled along. What really struck my attention at the time though was not the mess of the counters, or the untidy appearance of the floors, or even the unnatural coldness that one might find only upon death, but the unopened pie that sat on a wooden cutting block beside the sink. It looked quite delicious.

I began to rummage through the cabinets looking for a fork, my mouth watered, and I was starved. My stomach began to roar as if it were a demon; it became more and more agitated as each cabinet opened was revealed to be empty. Finally though I came upon a cabinet that possessed a single spoon.

I opened the pie and stuck the spoon into it with uncoordinated quickness, then shoved a spoonful of the cherry substance into my mouth. A smile began to smear across my face as the ruckus of my stomach began to subside.

As unsettling as it may be, while the roar of hunger left my stomach, I heard a new noise. The noise was not pleasant to my ears. I dropped the spoon to the crumb-littered counter as the noise grew louder by the seconds. Something traveled to my bowels; my throat dropped to my ribcage as my organs, lungs, liver, and kidneys all exploded out from my rectum. A hole blew clean through my gray sweatpants and splattered onto the unkempt floor signaling lights in the room to dim.

1. Welcome to Hell

The underworld is a place where few men intend to arrive. When a man pictures death, he pictures blue clouds and golden gates. A man pictures angels with harps and children laughing and playing. The underworld does not have blue clouds but the fog of ash that rises from the misery of men. There are no golden gates, only rusty fences circling pools of human waste. You do not hear children's laughter but the screams of guilty souls. Yes, this is the underworld.

I found myself lying on a sandy floor in the middle of what looked to be a titanic cavern. The cavern was lit by a red glow which webbed along the wall like spidery veins. The ceiling of the cavern rose maybe fifteen feet and was decorated with fissures and cracks.

Gripping onto a barrel that was near me, I forced myself to my feet, trying to figure out where I was. Slowly I headed toward a dark forbidding tunnel, but I quickly stood at a halt when a silhouette painted itself along the wall's surface. The sight of the shadow alone struck me with fear and sent currents of panic throughout me. The shadow was not of a man or of a woman. It was the shadow of a monster. The monster who owned that shadow was not someone I wanted to meet anytime soon.

"Why are you hiding?" A voice snuck upon me.

I spun around and looked up. I was face to face with the monster. Green hairs strung in front of his ghostly white face, his thick green lips moved as he spoke in a raspy-toned voice. He wore a tattered tan shirt and coordinating pants that looked to be a material I could not put my finger on.

"Why do you hide? Answer me, slave!" the voice asked again.

My eyes scanned the body looming over me. Standing at what I estimated to be seven feet tall, a lethal blade was grasped with his claw-like hands. Yellowish fingernails extended from the tips of his digits in an animal-like manner.

"You are not supposed to be here, slave; get back to the pits!" the voice commanded.

My body shivered like I was five men instead of one. I clenched my fists as the creature struck at me with the blunt end of his blade. I fell to the dirt as the creature proceeded to hand out a brutal punishment to my body.

"What is your name, slave?" the voice asked me.

I tried to think of my name as fast as I could, but nothing came to me. I so badly wanted to give him a name, any name, to stop the punishment I was receiving. With every kick to my ribcage I tried to shout out a random name, but I could not even make one up.

"Fine, you stubborn fool. We will see how you feel after a few decades in the seventh pit," the voice snarled at me.

The monster clasped onto my ankles and dragged me through the tunnel; rocks and pebbles from the ground snagged into my back as I was dragged along them. I lost my breath in astonishment as I was dragged into an even much larger cavern. Flames expelled from the ground as a thin bridge ran across a lake of boiling oils. Bodies filled the sea of torture, screaming endlessly in horror. Bruised, bloodied, and beaten men lay at the sides of the cavern walls speaking to themselves, mumbling babble under their breaths.

The creature that had pulled me across the stone bridge kicked me in my side before letting go of my ankles. Looking up as my nightmare advanced even more, a figure stood looking down at me. He stood on a flaming platform with a throne manufactured of human bones. The figure stood shorter than the creature that dragged me through the tunnels, maybe six feet, but he had a massive build. Black scaly skin covered his body, and he had beady red eyes. The most demonic feature though was the two horns that sat on top his head.

"I found this one in the Xeon cavern rummaging through barrels. He was attempting to escape pit duty and steal supplies. He also refuses to give me his name," the green-haired creature reported.

Lucifer stepped off the platform and approached me, looking me up and down. "I don't recognize this one. When did he arrive here, Lacious?"

The green haired creature named Lacious reached down into his garments and pulled out a scroll made of dirtied cloth. A puzzled look overcame his face as he peered down to me once more.

"Well, what is it, Lacious?" Lucifer asked.

"This is odd, master. Look at this." Lacious presented the shred of paper to Lucifer.

Curiosity filled my head as I tried to see what was written on the roll in Lacious's hands. Lucifer snapped his fingers, and as if they had it rehearsed Lacious reached down and grabbed me by my neck with a force that I could not grasp. He lifted me to my feet but threw me to the ground once more as if it were a game to him. He repeated this until Lucifer cleared his throat.

"Yes Lord?" Lacious asked.

"Step over here for a second, Lacious; I wish to speak with you." Lucifer turned his body a quarter from my sight.

Lacious growled at me as he approached Lucifer. I could hear them whisper to each other.

"Does he truly not remember his identity?" Lucifer asked, but I could not fathom why that was of substance.

"No Lord, why do you ask? Oh, you don't think this could be him do you?" Lacious replied.

"We may be able to use this to our advantage. Meanwhile, put him to work in the third pit. I want him at close reach."

Lacious nodded his head and turned to me once more. "All right—"

"Lacious, hold on!" Lucifer raised his voice, cutting off Lacious.

Lacious quickly turned to Lucifer and sighed in aggravation. "Yes?"

"Do not remind him of his identity. In fact, for insurance, bring him here to me," Lucifer commanded at which Lacious fetched me.

An emotion of doom overcame me as Lucifer raised his hand to my face. His fingernails extended a good three inches from the tips of his digits, and my face twisted as Lucifer carved into my forehead. At each carving into my flesh the room began to be overcome with heat. Not only that, but the cavern suddenly filled with unearthly, heart-wrenching musical notes of terror and hopelessness. My body fell to the ground as Lacious dropped me. Grabbing onto my forehead, I then looked at my palm and stared upon the bloody mess that had been made of me.

"Now he will be easy to find, hard to hide," Lucifer chuckled.

What had been carved into my flesh? Why was I of so much interest to them? Most of all though, what was my name?

2. The Seven Pits

The pit was nothing more than that—a twenty-foot hole in the ground filled to the brim with men of guilt. The pit was a mile long in width and was inhabited by three groups. The Slaves of Seduction were the first group and also the largest. The Slaves of Seduction were all the men of sexual sin—the pornographers, the molesters, and the rapists. You could call them the perverts of the underworld.

The second group were the Prisoners of Pain. This was a much smaller group of individuals. These are what people would call Satan worshipers. These were the men and women of earth who wished to reach Hell in contrary to the Heavens. Contrary to what they believed, however, being worshipers of Lucifer gave them no special privileges.

The third and most unusual of the groups were the Bellowing Bystanders. These were the unlucky losers of life who through their lives fell into evil patterns and lifestyles. They blamed their demise on their parents, their friends, even their mean third grade teacher. They blamed everybody but themselves.

As I sat in the pit, cushioned by a bed of rocks, I studied all three groups. The groups amused me; they refused to talk to anyone outside their own cliques. If this was by choice or just the nature of Hell I did not know yet.

I could hear them whispering. I knew they were talking about me since nobody else had anything carved into their foreheads and I assumed that was what they were discussing. Let it be noted, the worst part of Hell was not the feeling of absolute abandonment though, or the depressing music that filled the pits by a demon orchestra that no eye could see. It was the eternity factor. There was no issue of time and no sleep. There were no minutes, no hours, no days or weeks or months. There was only eternity. The only way to tell a concept or idea of time was by what were referred to as decades. A decade in Hell was not ten years as in life though. A decade was the time in between new arrivals to Hell. On a decade one of Lucifer's minions would lead a chained line of men into the bowels of Hell.

Each man would be thrown into the lake of boiling oils and tortured by Lacious and Lucifer. They loved to make men scream. Once they became bored with their victims they would throw them into the pits. Amazingly when each new arrival came they knew what group they belonged into. Not once in the decades I was in the third pit had I witnessed a new arrival entering the wrong group. If something like that were to happen I did not know what would be the consequence.

I was put to work in the third pit. The pits were split into seven sectors. The main pit being where most of us communed at was the largest of the seven. The second pit was on the parallel of the first; the second pit's floor was covered with broken glass and burning coals. A large steel door bearing the symbol of the goat could be opened from the second pit leading into the third. This once again was where I labored. Handed a spoon my only job was to dig—no place in particular, just to dig for all of eternity. I would dig for what could be considered hours or even as long as days for a living being. Then, with a sudden blink of my eyes, the holes I had suffered so much to achieve would be refilled with dirt.

The last four pits I had never entered and I was not urged to. I watched many men enter the path toward the last four pits and decades passed with no return. One thing was for sure, whatever lay beyond the final four had to be something more extreme than I could fathom.

I was on my knees constantly; after a few decades my clothes had deteriorated to nothing but a dirty skirt. My Caucasian skin had become stained a brownish tint. My hands looked diseased; thick layers of blood had embedded to my tattered flesh. Fingernails lay scattered around my labor space while bodily juices squirted out my fingertips at the most gentle pressure. My hair was matted and muddy, I had bloodshot eyes, and a broken nose and a broken ribcage were my trophies from repeated beatings handed to me by Lacious and his cast of minions. Yellow phlegm occupied my throat and was spat out when I spoke out loud. Overall I was no pretty sight, even for a sore eye.

Smelling of sweat and horse, the pit where I worked in repeatedly made me puke. With my rusty spoon in hand I struck the dirt, losing hope and soul with every strike. The carving scarred into my forehead had become a large purple scab that attracted attention from the other slaves who worked around me, the slaves who still refused to speak to me.

My eyelids tightened, my fists clenched while I struck the ground. I finally was about to lose all hope and I just wanted to give up. I just wanted to die, and the realization that I already was dead was so breathtaking a living man would have lost his mind. It was as if something indescribable had entered the very blood that ran through my veins and rushed my body's system, poisoning me. Then at that second, when I was beginning to lose it, I heard something. In a far off cry, a raspy voice that even demons cowered to, could be heard. The voice was shouting at somebody.

"What is your name, slave?"

I recognized the voice. It belonged to Lacious, but he was not speaking to me. In the decades I had been in Hell, not once had he interrogated a slave of his identity as he had done with me. For one he usually did not care. What did it mean?

3. The Stranger

After I dropped my tarnished spoon to the ground I raised my rear and crawled toward the cries. I sat there, my palms wrist-deep in mud, straining my bloodshot eyes to gaze up at the top of the pit. The voices dissolved into the dark notes that played relentlessly. Shaking my head I pondered if I had only imagined the voices all along. Perhaps I had finally lost it, finally gone over the edge. I had, after all, been down in the third pit for a while.

Turning my body around I slowly crawled back to where I had dropped my spoon. Mud collected to the skin of my knees, feet, and hands, making it almost look like I was wearing a suit of mud. I approached closer to my spoon when a sudden impact caused the spot to explode, leaving a small crater where I knelt. I wiped the mud from my eyes and looked over at a man, bruised and bloodied. He wore a white T-shirt covered in filth and ripped down the center, leaving it connected only by a few strands of threading. Bloody lines crossed his chest in clawed patterns, but the feature that caused my eyes to widen was that he had a number carved into his forehead.

The stranger apparently had been dropped from the top rim of the pit. A thirty-foot fall is painful even in death. The man who looked to be in his forties put his palm to his forehead, clutching his scalp with a painfully obvious migraine; his eyes opened and revealed a pair of emerald green spheres that in no way matched his exhausted appearance. He had a receding hairline, and surprisingly a sarcastic smile rose on his lips.

"So do they greet all their guests like this?"

Was he making a joke? Besides the fact that for the first time in decades words from anybody other than demons had been uttered to me, this man was speaking to me and he was trying to be funny. I tried to smile but it hurt too much. Instead I outstretched my hand, gripped his wrists, and with the limited power I still possessed, helped the stranger to his feet.

"Let's see here. Yes, very gloomy and scary. I could do without this horrible music though; do we have to keep it? Where's the dial? I could go with a little bit more pep." The stranger said while he looked sadly at his ripped shirt.

How could he joke? He stood with me in the third pit of Hell. The temperature was enough to make the sun itself sweat, and he spoke as if he could not smell the decaying flesh that surrounded him. The stranger turned around and looked at me now, concentrating a stare at my scarred forehead.

"Oh I see that you also have been touched. What is your name?" the stranger asked me.

I only wished I could answer him. His facial expression changed for a second as he gave me a cockeyed frown.

"What is wrong, boy? Has the cat got your tongue? Or perhaps a demon has it!" The stranger stepped closer to me.

Thinking hard, I looked to the ground. I had no name, or at least one I could remember. I recalled that I was addressed by Lacious once though as. . . .

"They named me Slave," I said.

I had not spoken in decades; as a result my voice sounded like an old hag with a smoking problem. My throat felt scratchy and each pronunciation I let leak out caused me pain. My answer seemed to please the stranger though.

"See now was that too hard? So Slave, what do you do for fun down here?" the stranger asked.

"Stranger, I don't know where you think you are. This is Hell, there is no fun. There is only pain."

"If there is no fun, then why do the demons laugh?" the stranger replied.

I was taken aback by the stranger's answer. I did not really know how to reply to it. Things were not becoming less confusing at all. As I looked at the stranger's forehead, I took notice of the numbers. Carved crookedly above his brow were the digits 989.

"What do the numbers above your brow mean?" I asked him.

"You have the same number, friend. You tell me," the stranger replied.

I shook my head and went back to work; digging my spoon out of the mud I continued my duty. The stranger laughed as he walked toward the wall of the pit and squatted down. If I did not know sleep was unreachable at death, I could have sworn I heard him snore.

I had counted more than three thousand screams by the time the hole I dug reached ten feet deep. Beyond exhaustion, I had to rest. Sitting cross-legged at the bottom of my little personal pit, I balanced my spoon on my nose. The hole I had achieved was something I could be proud of. Not only was it ten feet deep, but it also was four foot wide, and I had carved foot and hand holes into the sides so I would not have to claw myself out—a mistake I had made earlier in my first decade working in the third pit.

I found my breath ripped from my lungs as a finger tapped my shoulder. I had spun around in terror, but I was relieved to find it was only the stranger.

"I caught you sleeping on the job!" Stranger laughed.

"What are you doing, Stranger?" I asked him annoyed with curiosity.

The stranger rubbed his hands together as he sat across from me, also sitting cross-legged.

"I find it funny that you call me Stranger. You've not even attempted to ask me my name," Stranger said.

"What is your name?"

"You can call me Stranger." Stranger laughed and slapped my knee, apparently not knowing how bruised they were and sending volts of pain up my nerves, making my eyes water. Biting my lip I nodded my head and tucked my spoon in my waistband.

"Can I ask you something, Stranger?" I said.

"Sure, I got the time," Stranger said flamboyantly.

"I have been pondering this for some time since you have arrived. How is it that you can joke? You're in Hell, you know. Do you not find all of this frightening?" I asked the stranger.

Stranger rubbed his chin, appearing to be really thinking over the question. Finally, after a minute or so of chin rubbing, the stranger seemed to be ready with an answer.

"Yea, sure this place is scary. That does not mean you should be walking around like 'woe is me' all the time. Do not fail to realize that this place is just like your previous life." Stranger finished his mini speech and began picking at his nails as if the issue were closed.

"What do you mean?"

Stranger looked up at me with a smile on his face. His lips quivered as a layer of saliva covered them. His eyes glistened in a way I had not seen in a long time. They were full of life and mystery.

"Okay Slave, I'll break it down for you. In life you have free will, right? Well what makes you think you lose free will once you die? The answer is you do not. Hell is not only for failures in life; it is also for those in the spiritual realm who cannot seem to keep their act together. Do not think of Hell as an eternal place of torture; while it is that, it is also a prison, so just think of Satan as the warden," Stranger said to me as I took it all in trying to understand.

"I see. So we are in a spiritual prison, run by Lucifer," I said to Stranger, to see if I had gotten the facts straight.

"Run by Lucifer?" Stranger laughed.

"What? Lucifer is Satan," I replied.

"What makes you think Lucifer is Satan?" Stranger asked me.

"Who else could be Satan? Lucifer was the fallen angel, wasn't he?" I was becoming more confused and frustrated.

"Slave, what religion are you?"

"I was raised Roman Catholic." I smiled immediately, but only because I realized I had finally remembered something.

"Well don't you Roman Catholics believe God is three people in one being—the Father, the Son, and the Holy Ghost?" Stranger brought up a good point. "So what makes you think Satan is only one man? What makes you think he is not more?" A sly smile crawled across Stranger's face.

All this was news to me and a shocking revelation; could it be true? Was Satan a multi-being embodiment?

"Well Slave, I got to go. I have a party to plan," Stranger said.

"You're planning a party?" I asked with furrowed brows.

Stranger smiled at me as he began to climb up the hole, using the hand and foot notches I had made. I looked down at my hands; my skin was peeling over, revealing soft pink meat. My mouth was so dry moving my tongue felt like sandpaper running across the bottom of my mouth. On top of it all my head felt as if nails had been driven into it with a hammer. I had a lot of things to ponder. If only I could sleep.

4. Party Animals

I spent a while in the hole I had dug. Red smoke smelling of brimstone slowly began to fill the manhole. I stood to my feet and ran my fingers through my tangled hair. I began to climb my way out of the hole, pulling myself back onto the ground level. I gave a disgruntled sigh while attempting to stand to my feet. I looked ahead at all the other men and women working around me, I scanned the area for Stranger. Not being able to spot him, I pulled my spoon abroad and turned back to the hole. Had he really gone to plan a party? No, he could not possibly!

I continued for what would have been hours later if time existed. I had put my spoon down for a moment to wipe sweat from my face. Almost as if a work of magic, as my hand swept across my face a demon appeared before me which caused me to jump in alarm.

"Answer me now, Slave, why are you not working?" the demon shouted.

Not wanting another broken bone to add to my collection, I quickly picked up my spoon once more, but to my dismay the demon still took the opportunity to smash me in the mouth with his foot.

The demon was short and skinny. Mumps, bumps, and boils covered its yellowish body; a long scaly tail waved wildly behind him as he stared at me with green cat-like eyes. The demon wore chainmail attire, finished off by a barbaric-looking club.

The demon laughed with a cackle that was not unlike fingernails scraping across a chalkboard. He gripped his club with two hands; he raised it above his head and smashed it down upon me, splitting my lip in two.

"Go ahead, stop working. I would love to play with your liquefied flesh!" The demon cackled as he kicked me once more in my chest, knocking the wind out of me before running off.

Holding my chest in pain while taking a knee, I felt a hand rest upon my shoulder. I looked up to see it was none other than Stranger.

"Why are you not ever beaten?" I asked him.

Looking at me he smiled and patted my head. "You ask too many questions. Besides, who could harm this piece of work?" Stranger answered pointing to his face.

Spitting some blood onto the ground I wasted no time to grab my spoon and retreat into my hole. Stranger leaned over the small burrow and watched me descend while speaking to me.

"Hey, I think you will be happy to know that the arrangements for the party are almost complete. It's going to be pretty incredible," Stranger said.

Looking up from the bottom of my hole I continued my burrowing as Stranger kept blabbing on.

"I think I can get the demon orchestra to play some requests!"

This last comment was enough; I looked up toward Stranger, craning my neck. "Okay, now I know you're full of it. You're going to get the demon orchestra to play requests? I am sure Lucifer, Satan, the Devil, whatever you want to call him is going to allow a party to occur."

"What Daddy doesn't know can't hurt him," Stranger said before walking out of view snapping his fingers like a scene from a old musical.

My hole had become nearly forty feet deep when it happened. I could not believe it at first but the haunting music that played throughout Hell for the decades I had been there, and the decades before me, suddenly stopped. That was not the shocking occurrence though. What gripped my attention was what replaced the depressing chimes.

The bent, dulled-out spoon fell from my fingertips in result of my shock. My eyes widened, my ears tickled, and my toes curled as "Love Shack" entered my ears. As quickly as my broken feet could take me I emerged from my hole and crawled onto along the ground.

To my astonishment not only had the music been changed to that of more "pep" but also all three groups of Hell's inhabitants—Prisoners of Pain, Bellowing Bystanders, and the Slaves of Seduction—were all mingling. Men and women danced around; they laughed and chatted as if they were merely at their high school proms. The red eerie light of the third pit glistened in their eyes, and at the center of it all stood Stranger.

Stranger spotted me from afar and waved at me. A smile radiated from his face; his lips stretched disturbingly from ear to ear.

"Slave, C'mon over here, I have got a girl I want you to meet. Dude, she's got a nipple ring!"

I could not believe it. Not that the girl had a nipple ring, but that Stranger had pulled it off somehow. Trying not to swallow my tongue I started to walk toward Stranger and a woman who stood at his side. The woman stood about the same height as Stranger; jet black hair reached to the middle of her back, her eyes were ignited the color of gold, while she wore a tattered robe that gave brief flashes of her breasts when she turned the right ways.

"Slave, I would like you to meet my friend," Stranger said.

I scanned Strangers friend and tried to force a smile.

"Does your friend have a name?"

The dark-haired temptress gave me a sly facial expression as she leaned over to me, placing her lips on my ear and whispered, "You can call me Tasha."

Blowing into my ear, a shiver ran down my spine and down to my toes. "Would you like to dance?" I asked.

With a nod of her head I clasped onto her hand and led her out onto the dance floor. The dance floor consisted of burned sections of plywood laid out to form a giant square. Tasha pressed her body close to mine and moved with elaborate ease. Stranger stood back in the mingling area which was established a few feet from the dance floor. He stood there cross-armed and smiling as always.

Almost as if under the influence of a sex drug, my body became one of desire. My entire being moved along the dance floor with the temptress in my arms; we moved with the music that echoed against the pits walls. Tasha held me close to her chest and whispered a foreign tongue into my ear. With her running her fingers through my hair and brushing her hand along my back I nearly forgot I was in Hell.

The song ended though, and Tasha smiled and ran her finger along my neck and across my lips as she walked away looking behind at me teasingly. She had a cat-like strut; her body moved as if she walked on clouds.

A warm itch ran up my back, an itch that could not be scratched. I had the urge to follow the temptress; even as a new song began to play I could not take my eyes off her. With a glance over to the mingling area I made eye contact with Stranger; he stood talking to a few Bellowing Bystanders, and he nodded his head and winked at me. I knew what he was getting at and why not? So far he had gotten away with a lot of misconducts; it was about time I tried my own luck out.

People were everywhere, dancing tightly together like a massive orgy. Pushing, shoving, I bum rushed my way through the thicket of men, trailing a dozen yards behind Tasha. Although it looked as if I were going to be enveloped in the party that had grown by hundreds of participants since the last song, I was determined to catch up with my former dance partner.

Tasha would look behind and wink at me now and then, slowing down on purpose to give me a chance to catch up. She was almost within touch when I tripped over a fallen man. It was almost like a mosh pit, and it is a common knowledge it is nearly impossible to escape mosh pits at full action. Heels repeatedly crushed into my skull, I became a floor mat to decorate the plywood. Sandwiched in between the two distributors of pain, I put my weight onto my elbows, keeping my face from being smothered into the decaying wood.

A loud shriek, inhuman in sound, cut through the crowd. A fat, sweaty, hairy man who had stomped onto my ankles was suddenly plucked from the ground as if he were nothing more than a bug. A winged creature with orange skin that shined, giving off flame-like reflections, and which sported a large beak squawked as it whipped an eight-foot tail around. Large spikes made of bone ran down its tail like a ladder; the creature almost looked prehistoric.

The men and women who moments earlier were celebrating a party and dancing as if it were a mere night club now ran in terror, footprints stayed imprinted onto my body as I laid on the ground playing the part of a floor mat. People tripped over each other in a panicked effort to escape the pit now swarming with these flying monsters.

I quickly was filled with even more fear as I witnessed the flying monsters pick a man up off the ground; one monster clutched each side, and they ripped the man apart, silencing his pleas for help. The two halves of his body fell to the ground, staining the plywood a crimson red. Crawling over to the mutilated body I looked into its eyes. I could see nothing in its cold, dead spheres. It was almost as if he were not there, but how could that be? How can you be deader than dead?

The "pep" music that had been playing was discontinued; the only sound that graced the air now was that of screams and flesh ripping. Body parts fell around me almost like rain. The ground was becoming so filled with blood that as I sat in it the bloody waters came up to my ankles, staining my feet red.

The number of men and women in the pit grew smaller and smaller as the screams grew louder. I covered my face with my hands as I shook my head in deep dismay. I opened my eyes for a moment and caught sight between the fingers covering my face. Stranger was on the other end of the pit leaning against the wall cross-armed and smiling.

5. Soul Suckers

After the party was crashed, anyone who could still stand was chained in a single-file line along the pit's inner wall. Thick rusty links strapped our wrists to each other and our feet together. Sweat poured down our foreheads running into our eyes and down to our lips, giving us a bitter taste to our tongues.

The winged creatures that had swept down upon us now were perched around the top of the pit and watched us as if we could possibly move even if we wanted to. The single-file line stretched the entire length of the pit, and not one of us dared to move. The bodies that had been ripped apart during the raid lay in a dog pile in front of us maybe thirty feet away.

My eyes studied the motionless bodies trying to figure out what state they were in. Around that time a shiver ran up every man's spine that stood in that line. Lacious entered the pit from the large entryway leading from the second pit. In his hand he clutched a large red metallic rod which he rested on his broad shoulders. His green hair bounced with his long strides, he looked every man and woman in the eyes as he walked by them. When he reached halfway down the line he stopped for a second and turned his head to the pile of body parts and limp corpses.

Lacious gave the line one last evil glance as he strutted toward the body heap, gained his footing on a crushed skull, and climbed his way up the giant mound of rotted flesh till he reached the top. The top of the heap almost aligned with the pit's rim. He raised his rod and spoke down to us in his raspy voice which echoed along the walls in a cathedral-like manner.

"Are you all fools? You stupid pigs! What did you think you were doing? You are not on vacation at a park; this is not your family trip to Miami Beach. You will sweat, you will bleed, you will cry and scream, but you will not dance. I will listen to your bones snap, your backs break, the sound of your hope plummeting to the dark abyss, but I will not stand for your laughter or your insurrection!

"Do you all think you can do as you please? You are wrong! Now tell me who arranged this. Who made this be? Step forward or perish!" Lacious shouted to us all his lips trembled with fury.

I looked down the line and tried to spot Stranger, but I could not catch his face. Had he been a victim of the winged creatures' attacks? Was he in the pile of motionless bags of bones beneath Lacious's feet?

"Okay you cowards, keep your tongues in your mouths. I hope you enjoyed the party; it'll be the last thing you ever see."

Lacious's grip on the red rod in his hand tightened as he raised it above his head; casting it down, it struck the ground and pierced the dirt and was out of sight.

A few moments passed and our nerves began to relax but that is when the ground began to shake. We all became overwhelmed with anxiety and fell into each other as the ground began to crack open and steam rose from the fissured floor. Lacious laughed evilly as he snapped his fingers and a winged monster swooped down and grabbed him by its talons and flew him away, being followed by the rest of the monsters with wings.

As the floor began to implode on itself, the massive heap of bodies began to sink into the unstable ground, being swallowed up by an endless blackness. A scream I was not even aware was there emerged from my throat as the ground totally fell through and we all began plummeting down into darkness so black and cold it hurt the eyes just to look at it.

The chains broke off my wrists and ankles after a drop that seemed like it could have lasted for days impacted with some sort of ground which caused a giant crater in the darkness. In the darkness I just lay there not knowing if my eyes were open or closed. Suddenly in the distance I saw a light. Could it be? Had the heavens finally found some sort of flaw and come to fetch me? The light was starting to get closer now. My hopes were climaxing as thoughts rushed my mind.

After a good long period of time the light finally reached me, but after such a length of time in darkness even the feeble amount of brightness brought my eyes to a squint. A hand grabbed onto my arm and pulled me up. I could hear moans and groans of other men and women that lay around me, but I could care less about those miserable bastards. Still not opening my eyes, I was thrown onto the back of what I assumed was a horse and which began to move.

When I finally mustered the strength to open my eyes, what I saw was the winged monster that slaughtered the others at the party. I began to scream, but a hand wrapped around my mouth suppressed it. Shifting my eyes I saw that it was Stranger looking at me with a smile on his face, the smile I had yet to see him without.

"I'll let go if you do not scream, okay?" he said to me.

I nodded my head as he let go of my mouth; my dry, scabbed lips moved quickly as I eagerly wanted to gather facts.

"How'd I get here? What are you doing with one of those monsters? Why—" I continued to ramble but Stranger wrapped his hand around my mouth once again.

"Okay, shut up," he said.

As he let go of my mouth once more I sat up looking around at my surroundings. I sat in a small tunnel with just enough room to stand up in. The winged creature sat about ten feet away from me licking a rock and watching me out of the corner of its eye. Stranger sat back on a jagged rock and licked his lips.

Settled down I had grown used to having my entire body be one giant sore. I sat a few feet away from Stranger. I looked into his face; I had one main question to ask. "Stranger, are you an angel?"

As I finished my question Stranger paused and looked at me for a few moments before he slapped his knee and burst into uncontrollable laughter. After several moments he shook his head and answered me. "Dear God, Slave, I am no angel. I am in Hell for God's sake," Stranger laughed.

I quickly asked another question. "You're not here to rescue me from this place?"

Stranger shook his head as he continued to smile at me.

"Then how are you doing all this?" I asked.

"What do you mean?" Stranger replied.

"First you created that party then escaped the consequences handed down by Lacious. No man could do those things, and you have gotten away with them all. How? Hell, how did you get one of those creatures, whatever the hell they are?" I said pointing to the beast that now was licking its genitals.

"Soul suckers?"

"What?"

Stranger laughed and pointed to the winged creature. "It is a Soul Sucker."

I looked blankly at Stranger and shook my head in dismay. "Okay, saying I forgot my Monsters of Hell Handbook back home, how about you tell me what exactly a soul sucker is?"

"A soul sucker is sort of like riot police. Once a soul sucker devours a bit of your flesh he takes in your spirit. Think of it as sort of like solitary confinement, and don't worry about how I know this quite yet," Stranger said.

"So you mean all those corpses were not actually dead? Well I mean they're dead, of course, but that is why they were not moving. Their souls are now in the monster that ate them," I said.

"Soul suckers."

"Yeah, all right they're in the soul sucker that devoured them."

"Yes. There are worse places than Hell, you know," Stranger smiled and nodded.

"I got some more questions for you," I said.

"We don't have time, we got to get moving," Stranger replied as he began to stand to his feet.

"What? Where are we going?" I asked.

"You ask a lot of questions, you know that? But never the right ones. There's a reason I rescued you from the abyss; I need a hand in getting into the seventh pit," Stranger said.

"What! Are you crazy? Why would you want to get into the seventh pit?" I asked.

Stranger headed over toward the soul sucker, and I followed him closely behind. He hopped up onto the soul sucker's back and outstretched his hand, helping me onto what I must have mistaken earlier as a horse.

Stranger turned to me and pointed to the digits engraved into my forehead.

"Didn't you want to know what those numbers on your head were about?"

"Yes."

"Well we're going to find out," Stranger snickered.

With a tap of his foot on the side of the soul sucker, the creature rose to its talons and began to crawl low to the ground down the tunnel.

"Are we really going to the seventh pit?" I asked nervously.

Stranger laughed.

6. The Fourth Pit

"Get onto your knees, you bastard!"

Jack ordered his victim before he penetrated his ten-inch blade into the victim's neck. The man was clothed in tattered rags, greenish moss grew from his facial hair, and healed scars on his back were recently reopened.

The man could do nothing but scream. Actually that was his only option, for he stood on a platform at least three stone throws away from any form of escape. Blood sprayed out as the blade penetrated his collarbone; the man grabbed the handle of the blade to pull it out but only added more pain to his suffering.

The blade belonged not to a minion of Lucifer, not to some slackly demon, but it belonged to none other than Jack. You may know him otherwise as Jack the Ripper, or at least that is what Stranger told me.

The fourth pit, of course, lay beyond the third and was run by Jack. The fourth pit was a truly hellish site; it consisted of nothing but circular platforms maybe ten feet in radius. Each platform lay a few feet apart, and below the platforms a rolling ocean of orange plasma awaited. Many men had fallen into the orange substance, fallen into eternal suffocation.

Having traveled for at least two decades on the back of a soul sucker, the poor excuse for a wardrobe I once had rested behind me. Yes, I stood as naked as the day I was born. My lips had become so chapped that they resembled the bark of a tree; my hair was stiff and starchy. Over the decades my hands had became mangled and distorted, almost looking as vulgar as Lacious's.

"What's the deal with Jack?" I asked Stranger.

Stranger glanced over at me from the perch he squatted at; we were well above fifty feet and staring down. He had the same suspicious-looking smile on his face he had been wearing since the day I had met him.

"Back around oh, the 1880s there was a series of killings involving prostitutes. It wasn't the first serial killings really, but the first made big in the public and media."

"So that's all? I mean all he did was murder a few hookers?" I replied.

Stranger chuckled and continued.

"He didn't just murder them. Jack would go into the brothel and pick a woman, then while straddled over her, he would begin to strangle them. That's how he killed all of them, strangled them until their eyes showed white. Then afterwards he'd masturbate over their bodies. Sometimes he would cut out their sexual organs as a trophy. Oh yes, he was a truly sick individual."

Watching Jack below, standing over the bleeding man, I could not help but feel a bit sick. Just picturing him hovered over the corpse of a dead hooker and climaxing onto them made my stomach fold.

Stranger could see me holding my stomach as it churned. He placed a hand onto my shoulder and let out a sigh. "So do you want to ask him or should I?"

I was totally taken aback by the question. "Excuse me?"

"Well, we need to get to the fifth pit. How do you suppose we get there without crossing the fourth?" Stranger replied in such a nonchalant manner that it caused my fingers to go numb.

"Ask him what? Are you really insane? The guy killed hookers for shits and giggles, and you want to ask him for a green light to pass by?" I asked.

"Oh, I don't think he's such a bad guy."

"Not such a bad guy? He cut their genitalia out for trophies!"

"So?"

"So! Oh, I don't know, all right what do you want to ask him? Hello Mr. Ripper, may we please pass to reach the fifth pit? We really want to dig ourselves deeper into Hell?"

"Pretty much."

I had enough. With a sigh of disbelief I forced my fingers through my matted hair while Stranger shrugged and continued to stare down at Jack and the bleeding man.

"Fine I'll ask him," Stranger finally said.

"No, you moron!" I shouted while trying to pull Stranger back, but the grease and sweat packed onto our flesh made it easy for him to slip from my grip, as easy as a squealing pig.

Looming over the fifty-foot drop, Stranger placed his fingers into his mouth. If you asked me how he still managed to have any type of moisture in his mouth at all, I would have to say I did not know, but he managed to let out a horse whistle that a deaf man could have heard.

You would not think a simple arch of the neck could make a man defecate on himself, but as Jack looked up toward Stranger's whistle, I shit myself. A panic rushed my body while Stranger just looked over and smiled at me.

"I think he heard me."

I did not know what to do; the cavern walls began to spin as I turned as fast as I could and rushed back into the tunnels, leaving Stranger behind. Screw him, even if he had saved me. What kind of moron intentionally tries to get Jack the Ripper's attention?

Stones and pebbles became embedded into the flesh of my foot as I ran in a blind rush into the darkness of the tunnel. The coldness of the shadows laced over my body like a blanket of ice; not being able to see where I was, I ran face first into a tunnel wall, busting my nose open. I could feel the blood trail down my lip and into my mouth, and I could taste my very own blood.

I fell to the ground, hitting my head on a rock. I turned to my stomach and got to my knees. Standing to my feet, I no longer had any idea where I stood or in what direction I faced. With hands out in front of me, I tried to find the walls. Obviously though I was just walking the length of the tunnel, I must have gotten lost in my rush, for I was no longer in the enclosed tunnel Stranger and I had traveled earlier, but this tunnel was larger and more spacious.

I do not know how long I roamed the darkness. Eventually though I found a light, not some awesome glow of holiness, but a small speck of fire. The dried blood that coated my skin had turned into a hard crust from the coldness the tunnels had brought onto me. The flame was inside a small house revealed by the light of the fire. I entered the building but halted as I heard a voice cry out.

"Hello my name is Mary," a hidden voice said.

I was caught off guard, but there was no telling how long I had been searching the empty tunnels. I certainly did not expect to find a person though, let alone some woman.

"I said hello. My name is Mary Ann Nichols. What's your name?" the voice once again spoke out.

I did not know what to say. I decided to answer anyhow. "Hello Mary, they call me Slave. Where am I?"

"Tee hee, you're here silly," Mary said.

"Well, I know I'm here, Mary. Where is here though?" I replied.

"Are you a friend of Jack's?" she said.

"What do you mean, Mary?" I had no idea where this was going.

"You know Jack, silly, are you his friend?"

I could not tell where the voice was coming from. I spun around, or at least think I did, as a different voice spoke out from the darkness.

"Hi, I'm Annie Chapman."

There were two women there now. Maybe this one would prove more helpful.

"Hi Annie, where am I?" I asked.

"I'm Catherine Edowes," A third voice came.

The third voice sounded harsh and forced, almost as if the voice came from a disfigured jaw.

"How many of you are there?"

"They said there were only five, but there were many more."

"Excuse me?" I asked.

"He killed us all." Another voice presented itself.

What had I gotten myself into? I should have just stayed at the bottom of the abyss; why did I follow Stranger. Stranger! I had forgotten about him. I wondered what had happened to him.

"He returns soon."

My pondering was abruptly interrupted at this point. "Who's returning?"

"Jack, silly," Mary answered.

"What do you mean?" I asked her, my voice quivering.

Suddenly the small flicker of a flame exploded into a radiant flash and filled the space with an abundance of light. I was struck to my knees in both shock and horror as I finally was shown the faces that went with the voices that spoke to me.

I knelt in a circular structure; black walls filled with vexing fissures surrounded a flat sandy ground. Lining the walls were at least a dozen women nailed to the surface, disfigured and mutilated. Their genitals were cut out and bodies ripped apart.

"Jack, silly. He'll be home soon," Mary spoke from her spot on the wall, flesh hanging from her jaw line.

The rest of the room was very simple, the source of light came from the center of the room, and sharp metallic objects lay scattered about the floor and protruding from the women's naked rotting bodies.

"How soon will he be here?" I quickly asked, not wasting time to survey the room fully.

"Silly," Mary laughed. I gave her a puzzled look. "He's already here!"

Those three words caused my palms to become clammy. A firm hand was placed on my shoulder. I looked over at the bony, ghastly white digits resting upon my shoulder blade; I feared too much to look any farther.

"Welcome."

The welcome released from its lips forced me to gaze upon it. Jack stood there, maybe six feet tall, dressed in a proper-looking suit. Frilly cufflinks draped his hands as he released my shoulder to tip his top hat to me. I could not even force a scream from my vocal cords.

"What's your name?" Jack asked.

What is the deal with asking my name? I had grown used to it over the decades though and was becoming used to being called Slave.

"I am called Slave," I answered.

"Well Slave, I would like to welcome you to my brothel," Jack said to me.

I had not caught on very fast, but then it suddenly struck me. I suddenly realized why an entire pit was left to Jack. Why these murdered whores lined the walls, and why I was being greeted with a politeness that could make a python quiver. Jack the Ripper was running his very own whore house in Hell. Thinking fast, I figured it would be easiest to play along.

"Thank you," I simply replied.

"Choose any of them. Hell, pick them all if you want, boy. Do as you wish," Jack said to me as he winked and left after patting me on the shoulder a few times.

Jack vanished into a collection of shadows as I let out a sigh of relief; I thought I was finally out of the hole. To my dismay that is when the scary stuff really did start happening. I could hear the sound of flesh ripping from behind me, I turned around and goosebumps filled my complexion as the dozen mutilated whores ripped themselves off the wall, leaving parts of their hands nailed to the surface.

The ones with jawbones licked their lips; with their flesh rotting from their bones, they fondled their dry, scabby, carved-out breasts as they closed in on me. I pushed the first few away, but they overcame me. Attacking me, they gripped onto my legs and arms; the twelve slaughtered prostitutes tackled me to the ground and littered my body with their unwanted kisses and caresses. They ripped at my body, fingernails raking into my skin and taking samples for themselves. Mary and Anne laughed as they went down on me, biting into my tenderness and pulling on it, ripping the flesh from my bone. Blood was spat down my leg as Anne rose up, half my scrotum in her mouth. A few other girls bit onto my nipples and dug their claws into my ribcage. There were too many women to fight.

"Get off!" I urged them all.

Pushing them, shoving them, they would not leave. They kept on top of me, ripping me apart. I had to stop them, I had no choice. A gleam of an object caught my eye; I knew my only way out now. I let go my grip on one of the girls and grabbed onto a shard of glass lying buried under some sand. I struck at one of the girls, the shard of glass tearing into her eye socket, white liquid squirting out.

I wanted out of there so badly; I let loose and just wailed at the women, letting the shard of glass land where it willed. Blood began to soak the sand, and the bloody clumps of sand stuck to my sweaty body. I finally managed to get to my feet. I stood over the girls and did not soften my attacks on them at all.

"Die, all you damn whores!" I screamed while stabbing them all repeatedly. The women cried in joyous ecstasy as I riddled their bodies full of holes, repeatedly stabbing them.

Finally they all began to hiss at me and retreat. Not knowing exactly why, I was not going to complain. They all crawled back over to their sections of the rooms walls and waited. They stared at me and waited.

Crimson trails trickled down my forearm and biceps, curling around my naked flesh like snail trails. I could not believe what I had done; parts of my body as well as the girls lay scattered beneath my feet.

"I take it you enjoyed my ladies?"

I turned around to see Jack as he stood in front of me. He had sideburns that went over his cheekbones and directly connected to his mustache, but he had no hair on his chin. I stood bloodied and flesh clung to me that belonged to the whores. The shard of glass in my hand dripped with blood. He smiled and approached me, making me step backwards a bit. I did not know what to say.

"Well?" Jack asked as he cleared his throat.

Panic rushed my brain, as I suddenly thought that one usually pays for such things as these. I mean, what kind of brothel gives women away for free? The only problem though was that I had no money, or even knew what would be considered payment in Hell. What should I say?

"I'm sorry, Mr. Ripper, I don't have any money," I forced from my throat.

Jack stood there and stared at me, but then let out a deep roar of laughter.

"What?" I asked.

"You fool. You do not need to pay me. It is a gift."

"I don't follow."

"Those numbers on your forehead, you fool. I know what they mean!" Jack said before he disappeared once again into the shadows.

"Wait, don't leave yet!" I shouted, running after Jack. I couldn't believe it—what man in his right mind wanted Jack the Ripper to stick around so they could interview him.

7. Jack

I ran after Jack and almost tripped over dismembered body parts. I passed by the shadows, letting a chill rush my body. On the other side of the darkness I finally stopped my pursuit, finding Jack just a few feet ahead of me, standing on the edge of an old decaying balcony. The balcony leered over a giant canyon; in the canyon below men and women dragged rocks and wheelbarrows around, their skin peeling from their bones; long red scabs stretched their backs, scabs that made me cringe even from this height of perception.

Jack's back was to me; he reached into his pocket and pulled out a cigarette, then followed by lighting it with a match that he struck on the old balcony.

"You are still here?" Jack asked, still facing away.

"Yes, I was hoping you could help me with something," I replied.

Jack turned and let out a sigh that released a cloud of smoke that formed into the consorts of a skull. "Is that so?"

He smiled then tossed his cigarette over the edge of the balcony; it disappeared into the canyon as Jack began to walk away, his black jacket swaying in a wind that did not exist. I could not just let him walk away, I had questions I needed answered!

"What did you mean about my forehead?" I shouted real fast.

Jack stopped in his tracks. He spun his body around, the foot posted in the dirt created a small circular pattern under his foot. He took a step forward, and his eyes became alive. No longer were his eyes pitch black with no evident colors at all, not even a dark brown, but they had turned a burning red.

"Is that right? You mean to tell me you don't know what those numbers represent?" Jack asked.

I shook my head with coyness.

"Why don't you come with me, boy, and you will get your answers," Jack said as he paced toward me.

"All right, Mr. Ripper, let's go."
"Please, call me Jack!"

8. Nine Eighty-Nine

I found myself next in a small chamber. My fatigue helped in erasing exactly how I had gotten there from my memory; all I knew was that I was seated in a suede recliner.

The chamber that I sat in had been small and confined. Wooden oak walls were decorated by blurry pictures in bronze frames. The fireplace was roaring, fed only by what could be assumed to be bone fragments—probably from humans, I would guess.

"Hello?" I asked. I rose to my feet waiting for a response, but as I stood up my breath was sucked out from my lungs. I looked in disgust at somebody watching me from outside the window.

His skin was dark and discolored; what hair was left on his balding head was matted and thrown into different directions. The bloodshot veins in his eyes traveled past the eye sockets, across the cheeks, till finally they disappeared beyond his chin; his body was so bulimic looking skeletons would find his thinness alarming.

Stepping forward I asked, "Who are you?"

Then I realized something: that was no man outside a window, but it was my own image. I could not fathom the last time I had laid eyes on my own reflection.

I closed in on the mirror and placed my fingertips to it. I traced the outline of my broken face, a trail of blood painted itself onto the glass below my finger.

"I see you have occupied yourself," a voice came from behind me.

I spun around quickly to see Jack poking at the fire. One hand in his coat pocket, he then pointed the poker at the mirror I had been fondling. The end of the poker glowed red before slowly fading back to black.

"Oh, I'm sorry, Mr. Ripper. I mean Jack. It's just been so—"

"Yes, I know," Jack finished off my sentence.

"Please take a seat. I'm sure it's been a while since you've had one of those as well."

"Thank you," I said as Jack eased me into the suede recliner.

Jack walked over to the mantel and poured himself a glass of scotch while I once again surveyed the room. It all started coming back to me; Jack brought me back here by request. I was finally about to discover what the numbers scarred into my flesh meant.

"So, young man, you're probably asking yourself when I'm going to get to your question," Jack said while sipping at his scotch.

I nodded my head in hopes he would hurry and tell me. That is when I suddenly caught glimpse of the real window. I widened my eyes, not completely believing what I saw. The side of a face peeked into the chamber. Emerald green eyes and a sarcastic smile shone brightly—good God, it was Stranger!

"What's wrong?" Jack asked as he looked back at the window.

He must have seen me staring. I could not have him find out Stranger was eavesdropping. Stranger may be eccentric and a magnet for trouble, but he did not deserve whatever Jack the Ripper would hand out to him if he were caught listening in on a private conversation.

"Nothing, I was just thinking." I hoped he bought it.

Jack looked at me suspiciously before finishing off his scotch and tossing the glass out the window. Crossing the room, Jack's back was turned toward the window as Stranger sprung up into the frame holding the scotch glass and rubbing his head. I made quick motions with my hands trying to signal for Stranger to get out of there. Stranger just winked to me before lunging out of sight, but not in time to be missed by Jack.

"Who was that?" Jack snipped as he turned and faced toward the window.

"What? I didn't see anybody." I tried my best to try to cover but fell short of sounding confirming.

Jack charged the window, unsheathing a stainless steel blade from his cloak. I swallowed my tongue in anticipation, just awaiting Stranger to be the next notch on Jack the Ripper's belt.

"Jack—"

"Shut up! Sit down!" Jack cut me off, then forced me back into the recliner before he stormed out of the chamber door, through a giant red oak door that I had failed to see earlier.

From my comfy recliner I watched Jack the Ripper pass the window and go in search within the darkness in search of the person he saw portrayed in the chamber's window moments ago.

I stayed put in the recliner and picked at my scabs until a knock came to the chamber door. My ears perked up, and I leaned over, putting my elbows onto my knees in order to try to listen for more.

The knock came again, louder this time. My heart began to thump against my bruised chest cavity. A third time the knock came, louder and more aggressive than before; I managed to get myself to speak.

"Hello?" I whispered toward the oak door.

The bronze knob turned, and the door slowly swung open. My heavy heart continued to beat faster as five fingers appeared from the shadows and wrapped around the chamber door. The hand slowly opened the door, and the light from the fire slowly revealed the figure that stood in the doorway.

Standing in the doorway, a man of average build and average height stood. His brown hair was combed over his bald spot. A small rectangular mustache resided above his lip, and a swastika was sewn to his uniform along his arm.

"*Guten tag bin ich Adolph*," the man said.

I just stared at him; I did not know quite what to say. For one thing I could not even understand him, but it sounded German. As if the situation could not become more complicated, the foreign man suddenly was shoved farther inside the chamber; Jack now stood in the doorway, and his forearm tightly strangled Stranger who was blue in the face. Stranger waved to me as the German looked wide-eyed at everything that was happening within his chamber. A circle was formed composed of the German who clutched his uniform jacket nervously, Jack and the blue-faced Stranger blocked the only exit, and I sat in my comfy recliner.

"What the hell is going on?" Jack roared as he tossed Stranger across the room. The German scrambled to get out of the way.

"*Ich suche Jack die Trenmaschine. Ich wurde von Lucifer gesendet, um ihn fur Unterstuzung zu holen*," the German spat out as the three of us looked at him baffled.

"What is this moron saying?" Jack asked throwing his hands up in dismay.

"I think he's speaking German," I replied, to which Jack gave me a pinching stare that caused me to go coy.

"*Hast! Hast!*" the German said as he clapped his hands together.

Jack clenched his fists, his eyes burned red. I was sure they were going to charge each other at any moment.

"May I intervene?" Stranger placed himself between the two men.

Stranger cleared his throat and composed himself as the German and Jack exchanged glares.

"Before things get out of hand, why don't we all discuss matters first? I'm sure everyone has their own reasons for being here and I'm sure they're all justified reasons."

"All right, play the part of diplomat. Why are you here, in my chamber?" Jack demanded.

"*Ich bin konfus*," the German replied, but he was waved in dismissal by Jack.

"Please Jack, Stranger here doesn't mean any harm. He even shares the same marking above his forehead that I came here to learn about," I quickly said in attempt to diffuse the situation.

"What are you talking about? There is nothing on his forehead," Jack retorted.

I nodded my head but put that to a halt when I laid my eyes on Stranger. As I looked at his forehead the number no longer was carved into it. In fact, under closer inspection Stranger did not look that far off from the way he did the first time we met. After our time in the third pit of Hell and after we traveled through the abyss, he now stood in the center of Jack the Ripper's chamber with not even a smudge of dirt on his flesh. Why had I not ever noticed this before?

"Where is it, I don't see anything?" Jack said, closely examining Stranger's cranium.

"*Beeilen Sie sich Sie tauscht. Ich habe zu gehen,*" the German was once again clapping his hands together.

"Stranger, what is going on?" I mustered out, confused more than ever.

Stranger looked at me uneasily, trying his best to hide his forehead from me.

"My patience is growing thin," Jack snarled while once again unsheathing his blade.

The fireplace grew in intensity, as did Jack's eyes.

9. The Fifth Pit

Rusted bars enclosed Stranger and me. I pressed my face between the metal, breathing in the stale odor of tarnished steel. I was captured in a small cage, the type you might use for an oversized bird. To my left and right were two more cages exactly like mine. I focused my eyes to look to my left to see the German looking down and cussing under his breath; a great deal of sweat perspired from his forehead. Just then I noticed the bullet hole in his left temple.

The German's stare caused me to become curious as to what he was engaged at; I regretted afterwards, since I had now come to the realization we were strung at least a hundred feet above the ground. I tried to think how I had gotten there, and it suddenly all came back to me.

Earlier, inside Jack the Ripper's chambers, a large quarrel had broken out; Jack had knocked us all out and must have encaged us behind these bars. I looked to my right; Stranger, for the first time ever, was not smiling. I tried to speak to him, but only raspy air escaped my lungs; instead he turned to me.

"It's the fifth," he said.

I looked at him in confusion; he squeezed his cage's bars, and pressed his face almost through the bars, and suddenly a smile crept so slowly across his face I felt a chill dance up my back.

"Excuse me?" I replied.

"There it is! The fifth pit is right down there," he pointed with his eyes.

I was baffled at his comment. I could not understand, first off, how he would know where we were; second, did he not realize he was in a damn bird cage?

"Don't worry, I've got a plan," Stranger assured me.

"I don't think you understand the seriousness of the situation, Stranger. We're stuck at least a hundred feet in the air, and I don't know about you, but I have no wings."

Stranger laughed. "Oh really, is that a fact?"

Before I could get a chance to analyze his remark, Stranger began to swing his weight back and forth; his cage, like mine and the German's, was strung to the shadows by a thick rope. At every swing, it appeared Stranger was getting more force into his momentum, till he finally slammed into me.

"Hey! Whoa now, Stranger—"

I was cut off by another crash. I felt the bars vibrating; dust rattled from the top of the cage, and we banged cages a third time. This time the floor of Stranger's cage gave out and he went plummeting out of sight. His empty cage went flinging at me once more, and as it hit me, this time my cage's own floor also gave out! Screaming at the top of my lungs, blood and phlegm flew from my mouth as I fell a hundred feet.

Finally, after what would seem to be only a few moments, my body hit the solid ground with an impact that crushed my entire body like an accordion, and a large crater formed under me. Once the dust and cloud of smoke dispersed, I saw Stranger looming over me, reaching out his hand. I grabbed it, and he helped me up. I leaned over, coughing up some blood and what could be argued to be an organ. Looking up at Stranger once again, I noticed that he still had not a trace of dirt or blood on his person. I gave him an analyzing glare that he had to have picked up on but chose to ignore. I looked up at our two empty cages, which looked like mere breath mints from this distance. The German's cage was now swinging; he must have been trying to imitate our own stunt.

"Well let's walk," Stranger said as he began to shuffle off.

I shuffled after him, tossed my limp leg in front of me, and tried to keep up.

The fifth pit was much like a desert. The ground was black, and it covered everything, blending in with the shadowy horizon. The smell of sulfur and ash was absent, but there was an odor of staleness that existed. As we walked, I could not help but try to think of what we might run into next.

We walked and walked; if I was a living being I would say we walked for days. Stranger had not said very much though, and that was something new for him. He usually always had something to say. Eventually though, Stranger stopped walking. The entire duration of our walk through the fifth pit, I had been behind him, trying to keep up with my limp. Stranger turned around and my stomach sucker punched me, as I looked upon Stranger's face. His skin suddenly began to take a reddish tint to it. His smile was half of what it used to be. I remained speechless.

"I think we're lost," Stranger said to me in an undertone.

I just stared at his red flesh.

"I was certain if we took this direction we'd have reached the next level by now. Damn."

I just stared at his red flesh.

"Well, we can just keep moving in this direction; it can't go on forever." Stranger nodded his head in agreement with himself. He turned and began to walk once more, I dragged myself along, stunned to a point of bewilderment.

Something came over me; the closer we got, or the deeper into Hell we journeyed, the more changes were occurring in Stranger. I began to think back to our first few levels in Hell; he seemed normal—well except for his seemingly never-ending happy attitude. As we got deeper, he became more sober, and I recalled again in Jack's chamber the markings we once shared disappeared from his flesh. Now, here in the fifth pit of Hell, his skin was turning red and I had not seen any more dirt on him than the day we met.

I stopped my footwork, reached down to the ground, and grabbed myself a handful of black dirt. An urge came upon me; I wanted to find out what the deal with Stranger was once and for all. No stupid riddles or unfinished answers. Throwing the dirt at Stranger's back, it fell off his body, not staining his white shirt at all. Stranger stopped but did not turn around.

I bent down and grabbed some more dirt, crept up, and thrust my palm against his back, smearing the muddy substance into the fibers of his clothes. I was not shocked though to find it did not make a difference if I threw it or smeared it; it made no stains. Stranger finally turned his head to the side and looked at me.

"What do you think you're doing?" he asked me.

"Stranger—"

I could not finish my sentence; he quickly swung around and backhanded me. I fell to the ground like a bundle of sticks, my body limp and sprawled. Stranger grabbed some dirt and threw it at me, the dirt landed in my mouth and eyes.

"How does it taste?" he growled at me.

This was not the Stranger I had first met in the early pits of Hell; this was not the light-hearted man with a never fading smile. This Stranger kicked me in my broken ribcage, then ripped his shirt off, throwing it into the air where it unnaturally suspended for a few moments.

I stared at his red-fleshed body and found myself biting into my tongue. As blood trickled down the rim of my mouth, Stranger turned and a pair of titanic wings expanded from his back. They emerged from his flesh as if they had been hiding behind skin-toned camouflage. Dust began to rise from the black, cracked ground as a result of his flapping wings, while Stranger began to lift into the air and look down at me with an evil gaze.

I was horrified; had this all been a trick? Was this some demon sent to play games with me? I crawled away as fast as my broken body could take me, but I was soon lifted from the ground and picked up into the air. Stranger tossed me into the shadows, and my body hit with a thud, bounced a few times, and I glided face first in the dirt a few feet before finally I reached a stop. The skin on my face was peeled down, left behind, resting by my crippled feet. I slowly rolled over to see Stranger flapping his feathered wings above me; his skin turned a darker red.

"What are you?" I finally muttered.

"What am I? What am I? It's your fault I'm even here, you damn fool!" Stranger hollered at me, landing and bent down, I could feel his breath; it heated up the wet blood on my face and caused it to dry.

"I don't understand," I replied.

"Well, I'll tell you a little story. Perhaps it might educate you," Stranger said, standing to his feet and beginning to walk circles around my beaten body.

"Once upon a time there was a man. He was a good man; he didn't go to church or read the Bible, but he was still a good man. This man one day fell in love with a woman, but this woman wasn't very interested in him. You see, this man was poor, but this woman loved money; in fact she loved it with a passion.

"So you see this man decided he had to do something. On one night, after many failed attempts of becoming rich the fast and easy way, he was visited by the devil! This man was made a deal; the devil would give him many riches and would help him win the woman's hand in marriage in return for his everlasting soul. Are you getting the idea yet? Well, this man's soul became damned.

"God now was not very happy. He summoned the guardian angel of the man. The angel thought he'd be getting reassigned to a new human being; I mean what's the use of guarding a damned soul, he figured. But instead God tells the angel that if he let the man become damned, the same punishment was to be bestowed upon the angel!

"In other words, the guardian angel followed his human being everywhere, even after life. Even if that human went to Hell!" Stranger stared down upon me.

I finally managed to sit to my knees. Looking up at Stranger I began to understand. I was that man he was speaking about. I damned my own soul, and now as a result I dragged Stranger down here with me.

"But I asked you earlier, Stranger, if you were an angel."

"You fool, I'm not! The longer I remain in Hell, the faster I transform."

"I'm so sorry, Stranger." I closed my eyes and lowered my head.

Stranger closed his wings; they disappeared back into his flesh. Grabbing hold of me by my shoulder, he lifted me up and dusted off my back. I could not bring myself to look at him. He brought himself around, attempting to look me in the eyes.

"It's okay, you may look at me."

I slowly raised my eyes; the orbs once emerald had turned into a dull gray.

"You're going to make it all better. You'll bring us both our salvation. Both of us will be saved," Stranger said.

I looked at him puzzled. How was I supposed to accomplish that feat? Stranger eerily smiled at me before he turned to walk away once more; the release of his grip caused my body to slouch and fall a bit. We once again started to walk into the shadows, but after so many ordeals I could not find the strength to keep up with him. As we walked Stranger advanced farther and farther away from me, until he became a mere ant of an image in my vision and I was lost.

Finally he disappeared into the shadows of the fifth pit; I gave up and dropped to my knees. I covered my face with my hands, I begged for tears, but my dried-up tear ducts only scratched at my red, bloodshot eyes teasingly.

10. Lost

Abandoned by Stranger, hope, and a soul of my own, I forged on. Taking one step at a time, I continued to walk through the black desert; shadows beat down on my naked neck. The only bright side, if one could exist in a place such as this, was I had now learned two things.

The first was the identity of Stranger; the second was how I ended up here. I was a poor fool who sold my soul to Satan to become rich and famous. How clichéd is that, but at least it filled in some blanks. Stranger disappeared before I could find out my own identity though.

Something caught my eyes on the horizon. So adapted to seeing only light shadows, and dark sand, it appeared to be blurry and out of focus. I continued to hone in on the image, and soon the blurry figures appeared to be moving, yes moving around what appeared to be a fire.

The figures stopped, they must have become aware of my presence. I approached them slowly; my thin body crept toward them. As my eyes focused, I began to notice there were four men. All four men were round in shape, and they had long scruffy beards with meals still stuck in them. All but one of them wore a thick leather cap, and their eyes were dark and full of mystery.

"Hello, they call me Slave," I introduced myself.

The four men stared at me; their hands rubbed their disgusting guts. Veins bulged from their tummies and ooze collected around their navels. They continued to stare until finally erupting in bear-like laughter. I tried to laugh but only choked on the dryness of my throat.

"Welcome lad! Take a load off; you look terrible." Grabbing my arm, they tossed me to a seat; the log they sat me upon cut into my thigh.

"Thank you, who are you fellows?" I asked them, rubbing my bruised thigh.

Turning to each other, they continued their bellowing laughter, then they looked at me and smiled, before they took seats of their own.

"We are only the damned. We're on our way to the lower sixth! We've been out scouting new terrain; it is nice seeing new blood."

Interested, I asked the large men more. "You were scouting? Scouting for what, if you don't mind me asking?"

"We've just been on the search for—" The man stopped in mid speech. His eyes began to widen, and his mouth formed an oval.

"Lad, why do you have that marking upon your head?"

I reached up and rubbed the engraving while I looked at them sheepishly.

"To tell you the truth, I do not understand what it means. I've tried many times to learn its meaning but always fail."

The four men leaned into each other and whispered amongst themselves. One pointed at me, as the other smiled and, grabbing his belly, chuckled a bit, which caused it to roll. Then they turned back to me and leaned in, their beards almost catching into the fire.

"Those are the markings of the saved, lad!"

The fire caused an orange glow to envelop his face. A collection of spit that dried at the corners of his mouth sprayed out a bit while he breathed.

"That makes no sense—I'm damned," I replied to them.

"You're going to have to come with us, lad." One man rose to his feet, pulling a blade from his side.

Nervous, my body began to shake as I rose to my feet. By the time the other three had raised up, I had turned and began to shuffle away as fast as I could.

"Oh, no you don't, lad; you're mine!"

The fattest of the four grabbed me by the arm and ripped me toward him; my arm nearly popped from its socket and I screamed in agony.

"Don't harm the boy!" Another man shoved the one grabbing me.

"Don't put your hands on me, Horace!" My attacker shoved the one called Horace to the ground then landed a kick to his face. A tooth broke through his lip, and he spat up blood.

In a rage, Horace rose and unbuckled his britches, spun around in a clumsy fashion and whipped the other man in the face with his large leather belt. I used this opportunity to crawl away from the fight.

The two other large barbarians attempted their best to break up Horace and the other, not noticing my disappearance.

Covered now from my head to my toes in sores, bruises, cuts, and infected openings of flesh, I crawled deeper and deeper into the shadows. I could hear the four barbarians as they argued with each other in the distance, finally realizing I had escaped. I wondered what they wanted with me. Nothing added up; if only I could remember my life, perhaps I could piece this together.

Was I a damned soul destined for eternal torture? Or was there a bigger scheme of things? I could not do anything but keep moving.

11. Sixth Pit

Finally, I reached an end. Still blind to everything, I pressed the crown of my head into the solid wall in front of me. Slowly I continued to step forward, keeping my hands out to feel the smooth wall, and moved my feet slowly, not knowing if there possibly could be a drop-off.

I followed the wall until it came to what could be described as a ladder. My journey enabled me to collect some of my strength back, so I decided to ascend up the ladder. I did not have to climb too far before I found myself a platform. I grabbed it, and lifted myself onto it. Standing I then became aware that the platform led to a catwalk.

I took the catwalk, all the while paying attention to my surroundings. I saw that straight across the catwalk it led to a large round entryway. Torches lit the doorway from either side. A large six was carved into the door as well. I reached all the way up onto the door, running my fingers along the carving of the numeral six.

No doorknob was present, but there appeared to be a vertical slit down the center. The slit was deep and half an inch thick. Prying my thin fingers into the opening, I used all my existing strength to attempt to slide the door apart. It was a futile effort in the end; no matter how much force I applied the door would not budge.

Having given up, I released my fingers from the door and stepped back, beaten. I turned around and presented myself to failure when I heard a noise. The noise sounded like large stones being dragged across a sandy surface. Pivoting myself around, I looked upon the now open doorway. I almost lost my balance as a breeze of steamy dry air brushed by me, exiting from the doorway.

Looking past the circular doorway, a long wooden rope bridge extended a mile to a second side. Nothing but emptiness lay beneath the rope bridge, the bottom hidden by white fog. The sky was a light gray, with cigarette smoke clouds, and soul suckers were visible flying in circles around the structures that looked similar to old medieval castles.

I pushed myself to enter the sixth pit. Struck by a sudden heat wave, I had to adapt my breathing since the area seemingly was extinct of any fresh air.

I picked up a loose stone from the ground and tossed it at the bridge. As the stone contacted a piece of wood, the entire rope bridge shook, releasing a few pieces of plywood. I shook my head, gripped the rope on each side, and took my first step. Slow to apply all of my weight at once, I took another step followed by another. With my fourth step I could hear a crack, then saw a medium-sized fissure break into the wooden piece under my foot. Swallowing hard I forced myself to continue; I moved along the rope bridge, and my heart skipped every time I would hear a crack or break in the structure.

Having made it halfway across the bridge, I began to feel confident I would cross it with ease.

"Hurry along, you damn squab!" a voice from behind suddenly said.

I saw an old lady a few steps behind me. She was dressed in rags and smelled of toilet water. She glared at me with one good eye. The glass eye in her left socket rolled in circles as she squawked at me; spit flung from between her missing teeth.

"Sorry lady, I'm moving as fast as I can," I replied to her with a tone showcasing my vertigo.

"Oh malarkey, move on with it."

"Don't rush me!" I rebutted.

The old woman furrowed her eyebrows, and gripped onto the rope sides. Then with all her might, she began to jump up and down, letting loose a cackling laughter from her tar-filled lungs.

In mute response, I showed a look of fear and began to hustle. The old woman's cackle beating into my cranium, I tried my best to keep balance with all the shaking she was causing. I reached the last section of the rope bridge, but as I laid a heavy foot upon a piece of wood, the wood cracked down the center and my leg went through immediately. I remained stuck in the rope bridge for a few moments as my leg dangled like a worm being used as bait before the bridge around me snapped away and I went plummeting into the fog below.

Flung around like a rag doll, the fog coated my body with a watery residue. An empty scream escaped my lips and my head twisted in contortions so that I felt as if I would lose it.

My body finally landed into a body of water with a huge splash. I opened my eyes after shutting them at impact. I could see skeletons floating around me; body parts coated the waters floor, half hidden by moss. I just floated around in the water for a few moments before a hand reached from above and grabbed me by my upper jaw. I was pulled from the water and into a boat by a man looking to be in about his fifties.

Catching some air, I looked up at the fog and the dangling rope bridge.

"Welcome to the lower sixth," the man said to me.

I looked at the man who was clothed in a tunic and had graying silver hair and a beaten look on his face. His hands were stained with blood and he held an oar, I assumed with which to guide his boat.

"Thanks. I seemed to have fallen through the rope bridge above," I said to him.

"I just thought you wanted to go for a swim. My name is Cane, by the way," the man joked.

"Most people address me as Slave," I simply responded.

"That is an odd title to be addressed by," Cane answered, as I caught him suddenly taking notice of my forehead. His stare lasted a few moments, but then he acted as if not to have noticed it.

With a nod of his head, Cane dipped his oar into the waters and began to row.

"Where are we going?"

My question was answered once the fog broke from in front of us; I saw a village on an upcoming bank with huts made of sticks and mud. Men and women bustled around as children hit turtles with sledgehammers along the bank side.

The boat hit the beach, in which the moist dirt grabbed the boat in place. Cane stepped out; his bare feet hit the mud with a wet slap.

"Slave, can you tie the boat down," Cane said to me.

I nodded my head and grabbed the string attached to one end of the small vessel. Stepping onto the bank, I walked over to a stake in the ground a few feet away. While I tied the rope to the stake, I looked over at the children, their feet thickened with mud. One boy raised up his sledgehammer, the metal of the hammer's heads was coated with blood and chunks of shell stuck to it. Striking the sledgehammer down upon the turtle, the shell broke with a loud thud. The next boy took the hammer, and the turtle's eyes widened, trying to escape when the hammer struck down upon it once more. His tiny head went limp and some liquid bubbled from the fractured top.

Ahead of me, smoke rose from one of the mud structures. Cane entered the hut through an old rug being used as a door. I followed him and pushed the rug aside; the rug smelled of stale cheese and wet socks. Once we entered the small space, Cane nodded to me and motioned me toward the back wall. A woman lay on a bundle of dirty hay; she was missing eyelids and she reminded me of a porcelain doll.

"You can stay here if you'd like," Cane said as he issued me a cover as he exited the hut.

"Where'd you drop from, child?" the woman said to me.

"What causes you to think I've fallen from somewhere?" I asked.

"Well, you're soaking wet."

I turned to see the woman had leaned her cheek on her hand. She appeared to be naked, but her body was hidden under a thin sheet. I could see her hand move from under the coverings; she appeared to be stroking her belly.

"I fell from the bridge," I answered finally and quickly turned my head.

"Don't be so coy," she said.

Feeling unnerved I attempted to change the subject. "Cane seems nice."

The woman laughed, her lidless eyes caused her to look like a screeching owl. I forced a queer smile. "Yes, he's real nice. I'm sure you'll become like brothers," the woman cynically said.

Having spotted a washing bowl resting against the hut wall, I went to it. The water was not ideal for washing, some bugs had made sport of swimming in it, but I was long past any germ phobias. I dipped my wretched hands into the stale water and threw it onto my face. I rubbed the collected residue from my skin. I could hear the woman laugh; confused at first I caught my reflection in the murky water. Having washed the dirt from my face, I looked quite silly, and it looked like I had an egg painted on my face since the rest of my body was so tarnished with soil and sulfur, to which I had let a small laugh out at myself.

"Come join me over here."

I turned and the woman had sat up; the sheet had fallen to her lap exposing herself. She did not appear to have any shame in her exposure.

"My name is Slave." I stalled her request.

Just then Cane reentered the chamber, laughing at my face, then turned to his partner and ran a hand across her cheek while he walked by. Cane ran some water through his hair and then squatted next to me.

"You came just in time, Slave. The Festival of Ash is very soon."

"Disregard my ignorance, Cane, but what is the Festival of Ash?" I asked.

Cane shot a smile toward his woman, then stood up rubbing crumbs off his chest. The woman turned her smile to me.

"The festival is an old covenant the town made at the dawn of Hell. You see, Cane was the first man ever to be cast down here."

I looked toward Cane. He nodded his head with bragging enthusiasm.

"I made a deal with the devil; he gave me this town and reign over it as a sort of honor."

"Why did he do that?" I asked.

"I was the first to commit murder. I guess I impressed him, and my hands even still remain bloodstained. I still remember to this day how I was engulfed with rage and attacked my brother, killing him."

Stunned, I did not know quite what to say in reaction. "You killed your brother?"

Cane ignored my query as he moved onto another topic.

"Yes, well I hope you'll be happy to hear I'm making you the guest of honor."

"I'm going to be the guest of honor? What do I have to do?" I asked.

"Nothing special, don't worry, Slave. Trust me," Cane replied before exiting once more.

"Okay," I replied to his departing shadow. I did not know if I could trust Cane, but I had yet to find a reason not to.

12. Festival of Ash

The town of Cane was as alive as a blossoming spring. Men and women wore masks and makeup made of mud. Children fought in the streets, and drums were played at every corner. I walked through the alleyways and short streets, dodging children that ran by me, fending off street peddlers, and rejecting women's offers for their services.

The villagers had fastened logs together and, using archaic techniques, created a twenty-foot dragon. The dragon slid through the streets, operated by a dozen men hiding under the giant creature.

I jumped all of a sudden, startled by an explosion of fire in front of me. A thin man with stripes painted down his naked body laughed at me as he held a torch in front of his mouth.

Having finally started to enjoy myself, I shook my head and walked past the fire performer and began to search for Cane. I spotted him up between two huts; a large platform had been constructed at the center of the village square. Dirt and grime covered the spoiled wood as torches created a half-moon shape around the stage. Cane spotted me and summoned me to come toward him.

I squeezed my way through the crowd of people, grabbed Cane's outstretched arm, and he pulled me up onto the stage. He patted me on the back. We both laughed as I looked over the festivities; this was the first time I had seen such behavior since Stranger's party that was thrown in the third pit. Only this time I doubted Lacious would be around to bump heads with anyone.

"Right here is your chair, Slave!" Cane announced as he showed me to an elegant chair in the center of the stage.

"You own a chair?" I asked him with excitement.

"Yes, we have plenty of privileges in our town. Now please sit!"

I had not noticed until now, but the festival-goers suddenly had become more anxious. They began to crowd the stage, and many pointed at me. I made light of it though.

"So what do we do now?" I asked.

A figure loomed over the crowd and drew my attention. I saw a large bearded man wearing a leather cap. The man looked very familiar.

"Who is that large man who stands above everyone else, Cane?"

Stepping in front of my vision, Cane answered, "Don't worry about him."

I became alarmed, especially as I remembered where I had seen that large man before. Quickly I scanned the crowd looking for the three others. I spotted the second one leaning against a hut, the hut bending at the burden of his weight.

"I have to get going now, Cane, sorry for the—"

"You're not going anywhere!" Cane shoved me back into the chair as I attempted to stand.

I looked up at Cane; his eyes began to lose the friendliness they offered earlier. Tightening my grip onto the arms of the chair I spotted the third barbarian at the stage to my right, attempting to get his robust body over the edge.

"What is this all about?" My eyes thinned.

Cane leaned in as he placed his hand uncomfortably on my shoulder. The crowd of villagers became violent. I looked upon them, and their faces had taken a look of anorexia, almost like skeletons. How had I missed this feature before? Their mouths opened up, spit clinging from upper to lower lip, and they screamed at me.

"Sorry Slave, but you're going to get me what I want." Cane leaned in and kissed me on the forehead, but as his lips pressed against my markings he screamed. Grabbing onto his mouth, steam escaped from between his fingers. He yelled with a muffled cry, "Take him, take him!"

The oversized barbarian finally managed to squirm onto the stage; he grabbed hold of my shoulder, and his fingers cracked my collarbone. I looked over at Cane. He had moved his hand; his mouth had boiled up, and the flesh looked raw.

I thought fast; putting one and one together, I thought I had to try out a theory. After I grabbed onto the barbarians forearm I pressed my forehead against his chest. The barbarian screamed as smoke rose from his chest. Burnt hair could be smelled in the air as he loosened his grip on my shoulder. Quickly I turned to run, but my limp leg did not feel like cooperating, I went flying face first into the stage.

"Nice try," Cane said.

Rolled onto my back, Cane looked down at me loosening a chain from its coil. Blood spilled down my chin; I had busted my lip during my fall.

"Grab him, and do not give him a second chance this time, Victor," Cane ordered the barbarian.

Victor lifted me up, twisting my arm behind me. Cane wrapped the chain around my body; I felt my chest constrict, my breathing shallow. The crowd had grown crazy—children were lifted up onto men's shoulders, women kissed each other in brutal fashion, and the three other barbarians had managed to make their way onto the stage.

Circled around me, Horace and Victor held onto me while the other two stood beside Cane. The sky had turned charcoal; Cane raised his arms silencing the ocean of faces before us.

"Brothers and sisters, since the beginning we have been treated unfairly. Nothing we gave was ever good enough. At the beginning, I was banished to roam the land alone and barren. My children, who had nothing to do with the sins of their father, also fell under the same punishment! Is that what He calls fair?"

Cane delivered his speech to the crowd, and at his pauses they let out a roar of cheering.

"We were robbed once more of our own in the afterlife as well! Were we offered salvation or even a chance of redemption?"

The crowd all shook their heads as they roared, supporting Cane.

"No, till this day my hands are stained in my brother's blood!" Cane raised his hands to his face, then into the air. He dropped one hand swiftly to a gesture pointing toward me.

"Do not worry though, my children! Salvation may have refused us admission, but we have found our own ticket to redemption!"

The faces exploded with a rupture of applause and hollers, and I could feel the wave of hot air coming from their mouths. He was speaking about me, but I did not understand how I was their ticket to salvation.

13. Tribe of Cane

They placed me at the bottom of a dried-out well. Still laced in a thick corset of chains, I was a prisoner of the shadows.

"Hey you, look up here!" a voice said from above.

I looked up to see a boy smiling down at me. The charcoal sky moved behind him as he held a rock out in front of him. He saw me look up, then with a wink of his eye the boy dropped the rock. The rock plummeted down and missed my head but made a direct hit with my big toe. My toe snapped at the impact but was deafened out by my scream.

The boy laughed to himself as he blinked his freckled eyes. I recognized him from the beach when I first arrived. Confused, the strength I had finally collected was quickly escaping my clutches. I could do nothing but stare at the dim outline of bricks that surrounded me, attempting to make pictures from the slime that covered them. It was almost as if they were some kind of inkblot projection tests to me.

Horace, one of the barbarians, returned eventually. I knew he arrived when his large figure eclipsed the only light established to my prison dwelling.

"Hello lad, you're looking good," Horace said in a light Irish tone I just now picked up on.

A chain was lowered into the well with an ugly hook attached to the end. Horace above tried to maneuver the hook, attempting to snag my bindings. Finally, after plenty of hassle, the hook snagged me. Horace cleared his throat and wrapped the end of his chain around his forearm a few times then began to pull me up.

The bindings around me tightened as I felt my body lifted from the ground. My back cracked a few times by the time I was pulled a quarter of the way up. Horace suddenly sneezed and I was dropped; quickly reestablishing his grip, my body whiplashed forward, causing my knee to hit the well wall and nearly busting it apart. With clenched teeth, Horace pulled me from the well and onto the pebbled dirt.

Even the small amount of light in the sky burned my eyes, causing me to squeeze them shut. Temporarily blinded I could only feel Horace lift me to his shoulders and carry me off.

As I was carried through the streets of Cane's village, I could hear people's voices pass me by. At a few turns, my head was knocked into the side of a hut or market stand. Slowly my vision returned to me, and now I opened my eyes to see the macabre of the town.

Dressed in dirty sheets, an old man with a long, prominent nose bit into a moldy fruit. The juices rolled down his chin and spilled to the ground where a wet dog licked it up. A few children held down a young woman, while a few older women clapped and laughed.

We passed a larger hut; inside I saw Victor and the other two barbarians taking turns throwing pigs. Finally as we reached Cane's home near the beach, Horace dropped me. My neck hit the ground first, and my body landed harder than usual due to the heavy chains cast around me.

As I laid there coughing Cane stepped out from his hut. He towered over me, but I paid more attention to his woman who peeked out from behind their imitation door.

"Bring him inside," Cane simply said.

Cane stepped back into his hut, and Horace sighed as he turned around, grabbing my ankles to drag me inside. After Horace lifted up the entry's drape, it flapped back down, hitting me in the face and giving me a nasty taste of mold.

I was thrown onto the bed of hay the woman was relaxing on the last time I was in there, then Horace took a seat near the exit. Cane stroked his cheeks with both hands, closed his eyes, and ran his fingers through his hair.

I decided it was time to finally get some answers.

"What is going on Cane?" I asked.

Cane's complexion had turned pale since the last occasion I saw him, and red marks were across his chest as if he had been having a case of nervous itching.

"Stop playing the part of a fool, Aziel," Cane said while not looking me in the eye.

His words went over my head at first but then put me in a state of shock. "What did you call me?"

"Aziel, your name is Aziel, and I do not understand the games you are playing. Everyone from the damn abyss to the seventh pit of Hell knows what those markings on your forehead mean, but you're telling me you don't?"

"No I don't," I said.

"You don't! You don't! You are a liar!" Cane yelled.

The room started to grow tense; the woman hid herself in the corner of the room, and Horace kept his mouth closed while Cane's face boiled red. I myself began to lose temper as well. I could feel a rage build inside me, and before I knew it I exploded with anger.

"You wonder why salvation was never offered to you, Cane? It's because you have an evil soul! If you know so much about the markings on my head, why don't you share them? It would be a relief to finally know what it means!" I hollered as spit flew from my trembling lips.

A moment of silence engrossed the room. Nobody dared to speak nor break the silence—that was, until Horace spoke. "He thinks you have a soul, Cane."

I closed my mouth after realizing it had been hanging open the entire time. Horace had a sober expression on his face, and Cane looked down at the ground with his shoulders shrugged in defeat.

"That's what the markings mean, Aziel. That you have a soul."

"I don't get it," I replied. "Lucifer is the one that carved them into me. Also how would you explain—"

"Yes, Lucifer gave you your soul back. That was always the deal," Cane said before sitting to the floor.

"That was always the deal? I know I sold my soul to the devil for richness and fame, but why would he give me my soul back?"

"That's just the half of it, Aziel. From the very beginning it was planned. You see, when Lucifer was first cast down from Heaven, he was forbidden ever to return. Much like I was. That is why there's never been an attack on Paradise, you see; it's impossible for the damned to enter." Cane rubbed his face.

"So how does that explain how I fit in?" I asked.

Cane looked at me and continued. "If it weren't for you selling your soul, you'd have gone to Paradise. If you were to be given your soul back, you could breach Heaven's gate, opening Paradise for anyone. Anyone would include Lucifer as well and all of Hell. The plan was simple: you were to die and when given your soul back we'd send you to Heaven. Once the gates were open, all of Hell was to attack and sack Paradise, taking it for ourselves."

The information came in so fast it was difficult to process. My head began to ache while I figured out my situation.

"If that's all true, then why am I chained up right now instead of on my way to Heaven? Shouldn't I like disappear or beam up or something?"

"It doesn't quite work like that," Cane answered.

Horace rubbed his tummy, causing it to shake. "Takes more work than that, lad."

"Well don't you two want to go to Paradise? What was all that talk about revenge earlier?" I asked.

"Lucifer doesn't deserve to attain such a victory. The ultimate slap in the face ever would to succeed where he could not. That is why you're going to help us, not him. If you truly forgot your name, that would make sense as to why he hadn't sent you already on your way," Cane said.

"What would that have to do with anything, and how do you know my name is Aziel?"

"It takes more than a soul to open Heaven's gate; you need to also have a name. As for how I know all this, when you've been in Hell as long as I have, you obtain resources. I've known about you since you signed your soul away. Never thought I'd have an opportunity like this though, until you dropped near my boat."

We all shared a laugh for a second before returning to silence. Cane stood to his feet and walked over to me, snapped his fingers, and ordered to Horace, "Unchain him, Horace. I guess after all this I can make you an offer. I apologize about the treatment earlier, but you must understand I had to make a statement to my people. I'm offering you a deal though; you can work with me by my side or stay chained up like a monkey," Cane said while extending his hand to me.

Horace finished untwisting the chain from around my upper torso but held it ready in case I made a rash decision. Victor and the other two barbarians could be heard enclosing on the hut, laughing and joking. I eyed the room once more before I extended my hand to give Cane a handshake. I could not help but feel I had just made a deal with the real devil.

14. A Strange Turn

I learned later that the other two barbarians were named Ivan and Shaun. I also learned later on they loved to play a game involving pigs. They would take turns tossing a pig, and how it landed would determine how many points they would receive.

Cane and I were seated at a wooden booth. The wood squeaked at any movement we made and had a glue-like residue plastered all over it. Horace sat next to me; his large arms hid me from sight, resulting in me having to peek over his biceps to speak with Cane.

A pig flew across the room and smashed a drunken old man to the floor. Victor roared with laughter.

"Sorry mate, but that did not count!"

"Yes it did, you bloke! She landed on her backside!" Ivan retorted.

"She hit Larry. She doesn't count!" Victor laughed.

Ivan picked up the pig in anger and threw it at Victor. Victor ducked his head, so the pig landed headfirst into the wall, breaking its neck.

"See what you've done now, Ivan. You killed our pig!" Shaun slapped Ivan on the back of his head.

"Oh, shut up, Shaun. We've got another," Victor laughed while patting Ivan on the back.

Horace laughed at the men before Cane snapped his fingers to get his attention. Horace's arm smelled so raw that the skin on my nose began to feel numb. A wet sweat dripped from his pits and I feared to even come near contact with it.

"Now do you understand the plan, Aziel?" Cane asked me.

I stared off into space for a while before realizing I was being spoken to.

"I'm sorry, Cane. I just am not used to being called Aziel."

"That's understakable. So do you understand?" Cane interlocked his fingers, waiting for me to respond.

"I'm going to the seventh pit with Horace, Victor, Ivan, and Shaun. What I don't understand is how you expect to get past Lucifer's radar. Also how I'm supposed to even reach Heaven," I said.

"You don't need to worry about it," Cane answered.

I peeked up from behind Horace's shoulder and saw Cane looking toward the broken cedar table.

"Why shouldn't I worry? What aren't you telling me?"

"Well we don't really know how to either," Cane replied.

"Don't worry though, lad, we know what we're doing," Horace nudged me.

"You know what you're doing? You don't know either, you just said. Are you serious?" I said in disbelief.

"Calm down, Aziel, you're all going to keep a low profile. Anyways, Lucifer tends to hang around the first few pits anyway. He enjoys the fresh ones."

I rolled my eyes in contempt.

"Whatever you say, Cane; I just don't see how you expect these guys to keep a low profile."

"What do you mean?" Cane asked before a pig was hurled onto our table, breaking the cedar in half.

"Two points for you, Ivan!" Horace laughed out loud.

We finished up our business and headed toward the bank where the barbarian's ship was ported. Women and children had retired to their homes; the streets were deserted and stale. As we walked down the street, I saw the freckled boy from earlier with his head poked around a corner. He quickly dodged my glance and ran away laughing. Shaun and Ivan argued as they straggled behind Horace and Victor.

Cane walked next to me, speaking under his breath. "I know you're nervous still."

I looked at him and smirked. "No, I'm fine."

"Your hands are shaking like a three-year-old's," Cane answered back.

I leaned in toward Cane, trying to think of words to say. He patted my back in reassurance. "Just stick with the boys and you'll be fine."

Feeling confused and distraught I slowed down my pace, allowing Horace to cut in on my conversation with Cane. The sky mocked me as it rolled by making faces. After reaching the bank, I looked at the ship I was supposed to board—an old Viking ship that was missing large chunks of wood, the sail was tattered into pieces, and the goddess carved in the front was decapitated. The stale bank waters tossed the ship about like a toy. I could only imagine the look on my face was that of distress, but after looking at the barbarians I felt a bit more relaxed. Their faces shined with pride.

"There she is, lad; what ya think?" Victor asked me, while weighting down his arm around me.

"She's beautiful," I lied.

"You're not taking her," Cane stepped in.

Victor's mouth dropped as he took a step toward Cane. I could feel Horace and Ivan tensing up as well. Cane sighed and pointed toward the ship.

"It's too large Victor. Even a blind nomad could see that coming!" Cane told Victor and his men.

Shaun and Ivan began to make noises I could only associate with being disgruntled. I personally felt relieved at not having to ride such a riddled ship.

"What do you expect us to take then?" Victor hollered as his arms rose up in a wing-like manner.

Cane smiled sadistically as he strolled into his beachside hut and disappeared inside to come back out with an oar. He had to be joking.

Next thing I knew I was a sardine between the four barbarians; the five of us were crammed into Cane's small canoe. The heavy sum of us caused the boat to submerge partially. Yellow water came to the brim of the ship, spilling in at random times. The collected smell of the four brutes was almost as unbearable as the folksongs Ivan and Horace were singing.

The small boat carried us downstream for miles; dead woodland was on both sides of us. Old trees with no leaves danced in the hot breeze. Fire was present on any brush that was still alive and well. After the first few miles, though, I began to relax. I craned my neck up and watched the clouds spin along the horizon.

As if I was in an altered state, I was snapped right out of it as the boat crashed to a stop. The boat had hit a large rock that was in the center of the stream.

"How did you manage to do that?" I said in disbelief.

"Sorry, I did not see it," Victor answered, shying his face.

"You are right, Victor; that was not there earlier," Ivan said to Victor but addressed it to us all.

"Can we go around it?" I asked.

I waited for a reply but the barbarians were all silent. Their heads began to spin around, eyes scanning the tree line on either side of us.

"What is it? What are you looking for?

Shaun motioned for me to be silent as he tapped Horace on the shoulder. The four barbarians' attention became directed to a single tree on our left flank. My eyes had to be lying to me. Behind an old ash tree, a tail waved around wildly. I felt myself scooting back, almost falling overboard. I attempted to say something, but Horace grabbed my mouth, his hand overwhelming my face.

"Horace, this is Cane's land. Demons aren't allowed to cross into the lower sixth," Shaun whispered.

"Don't be foolish, Shaun. They can do whatever they want; they just usually don't have a reason to," Horace responded, finally releasing my face from his clutch.

Ivan and Shaun exited the boat, and our boat bounced at the sudden loss in weight. The two barbarians disappeared into the waters but reemerged later at the bank. Bodies drenched and dripping, the two men slowly made their way toward the tree hiding our unknown visitor. By the time they had come within four feet of the trunk, an enormous pair of bat-like wings expanded and the demon exploded through the tree trunk. Timber flew everywhere, crashing into the water and causing our boat to turn over.

Under the water, I attempted to swim back up but was struck in the head by the bobbing boat. Horace was at the stream's bed, throwing his limbs around. I guess he could not swim. There was no way I could lift a man his size to the surface, so I saved myself. I grabbed onto the rock we crashed into and pulled myself above water. Bent over I rubbed the water from my eyes, and with my vision cleared I looked around. Horace was still on the bottom of the stream bed, and the three other barbarians were suspended in the trees. One of the branches broke, and Ivan fell from his perch, hitting every branch on his way down. I quickly spun around to look for the attacker. The area was deserted; I could not see any presence but my fallen chaperones.

Thinking maybe it had retreated, I found that to be only a desperate hope as I turned around to see the flying demon torpedoing toward me. I did not have time to scream, the open-mouthed demon clutched onto me by its claws and went spinning into the sky.

I looked below to see Horace emerge from the water and gazed in disbelief as I disappeared into the clouds above.

I got my first close look at my abductor in the sky. His skin was dark red and hard like tree bark. His face was thin yet chiseled, and his eyes were a dull gray. The wings that carried us through the air previously looked like bat wings, but they suddenly appeared to be feathered and colored midnight blue.

Blinded by the thickness of the clouds, I had no idea where it was taking me. Eventually the clouds broke, and the destination was revealed. The sky had changed from the charcoal gray and now was a golden orange. Fire randomly exploded from hot springs, and thousands of people crawled around the ground just moaning in agony.

The stench of burnt flesh brushed against my cheeks, and as the demon flew us at a lower altitude, screaming individuals reached up trying to grab onto my body. I closed my eyes, not wanting to see any of what was transpiring. With eyes closed, I suddenly felt released into the air. My body flew and impacted against a wall, bouncing me to a rough surface.

Slowly I allowed my eyes to open. It appeared I was inside a cave; straight ahead was the circular exit, and the demon that abducted me stood in front of it. He tapped his foot and retracted his wings to his back.

"So I guess you got me," I said to the demon, accepting defeat.

I figured Lucifer had finally sent for me. Now it was time for my reckoning. I continued to feel more anxious as the demon just stood there and stared at me.

"Do you have any idea how long it took me to find you?" the demon finally said.

My eyes flinched when I finally realized who the demon was. Slowly I stood to my feet, dusting off my body. Stepping back against the wall, I slowly pronounced his name.

"Stranger, is that really you?"

It stepped forward, then raised its index fingers to his cheekbones to signify dimples.

"That's right, the one and only."

"What happened to you? You look so different!" I could not believe my eyes. "Where are we?"

"The upper sixth; you know what is funny, Slave? I reached all the way to the seventh pit before I realized you weren't behind me anymore. I know I may have been a little, let's say strong-handed, but I did not think you'd run away."

"Stranger, I didn't mean to. I tried my best to keep up, but I just lost you." I approached Stranger, but then stopped as I saw his eyes.

"Where did you go?" he simply replied.

I did not know what to say. Would it have been wise to tell him everything I had learned? I decided just to tell him as much as I needed to.

"I found the Tribe of Cane."

Stranger's eyes widened, and the purple scaly bags under them darkened.

"You met Cane?" Stranger turned his head away from me. "What did he want from you?"

I was about to reply when Stranger cut me off abruptly. "No, don't answer that. It's not relevant anymore. I do assume, though, he told you about the rest of your deal?"

"Yes," I replied.

"I figured he'd know about that. The devil didn't give him his own town just because he was impressed at his invention of murder. It was mainly to get that damn goat's nose out of his business."

I nodded my head and walked up to the cave's exit. There was a drop-off of at least a thousand feet. From this point the crawling bodies appeared to be grains of pepper, blowing in the wind.

"So are you going to turn me in now?" I asked Stranger.

Stranger turned, his jagged teeth appeared as he smiled.

"No. Like I said earlier, you're going to get me out of here. If I wanted to be a demon I'd have joined Lucifer when he first rose up. It's incredibly hard; I've grown an internal hunger for destruction. The longer I'm here in Hell, the more damned I become."

Stranger was hidden by shadows. His head drooped down, and his wings lay limp against the floor. I felt truly sad for him; after all, his damnation was partially my fault.

"I really am sorry, Stranger." I wanted to reassure him by touch but feared even being near him.

Stranger lifted his head and with a fading smile spoke. "Sit down, it's time I told you something."

Eager to maybe learn something new, I hurried to the opposite wall. Lowering myself to the floor, I pressed my back against the cave wall as Stranger's chest heaved and he told me his story.

"Now listen to me, Slave—"

"Aziel!" I cut off Stranger. "I know my name is Aziel."

Stranger looked alarmed. His eyes widened as he replied, "No it is not. Where did you hear that name?"

"Cane told me. He told me all about the deal."

"No, I'm afraid he was wrong. I am Aziel," Stranger answered back.

I shook my head, not understanding. "No, I am confused."

"What I told you earlier was partially true," Stranger continued. "I may have twisted the facts around, though."

"How is that so?" I replied.

"Well it may not have been you that made a deal with the devil. It could have been me."

Not knowing what to say, I just let Stranger finish talking.

"I've been behind it all. I was sick of having no freedom. I had to protect humans who, after they sinned all their lives, could share the Heavens with us angels, who were the original creations. Heaven belonged to us, but then humans received both—life on earth and afterlife in Paradise. It sickened me.

"For thousands of years I had that chip on my shoulder. So I finally broke down. I knew that Satan couldn't enter Paradise or even speak to the creator. Only a soul can open the gates of Heaven. Knowing we're tied together, I sold you out to Satan. I erased your memory and I'm the one who murdered you. Everything after that was also set up—my sudden arrival, the party I manifested.

"The plan was after Lacious sent you and the others into the abyss, I would rescue you and lead you to Paradise. Once the gates opened, all of Hell would be ready to storm in and siege Heaven for ourselves. I would finally get my home back."

Stranger finished what he had to say, then bowed down his head in shame. I was betrayed by my own guardian angel. I shot up and speared Stranger against the wall. He looked up at me in shock, as I landed a right hook across his jaw. At the impact of my punch, my hand felt like it busted apart. I fell backwards, holding my swollen fist to my chest. Stranger stood over me, his wings tucked in. He stretched out his hand to help me up.

"So you see, Slave, I'm the one who's sorry."

15. Lacious

Curled up at the back of the cave, I did not want to be near Stranger. Stranger leaned against the wall, looking over the edge. I turned my head to look at him, choosing my words wisely. "So now what happens? Was this part of your plan too?" I asked.

Stranger did not turn to me. He just looked forward.

"Answer me, Stranger! Was this the next step in selling me out?"

I heard Stranger mutter something, but it was soft and under his breath.

"What?" I asked him to repeat himself.

"No. If I was following the plan, we'd be at Heaven's gates by now. I went against orders," Stranger replied, finally turning from his dead stare.

Before I could question Stranger on what he just said, he continued to talk. "That's one thing about humans. You all can make as many mistakes as you wish, and it's always all right. Can't I make one as well?"

"Stranger, you didn't just lust after your neighbor's wife—you sold me out to Satan!"

"All right, it was a bit bigger of a mistake," Stranger chuckled.

"So what do we do now?" I finally muttered after some silence.

"It turns out that Lucifer wasn't too happy about my change of plans."

"I bet that's an understatement," I replied.

Stranger smiled again, while he turned away from the cave entrance and approached me. "Right now, he's probably got three legions looking for you."

The thought of three legions after me, looking under every nook and cranny, deeply disturbed me. I brushed my feet off and stood by Stranger's side.

"Three legions, you say? Well then there is Cane. He wants to overthrow both sides."

Stranger let loose a deep laughter and slapped me on the back, nearly knocking me over the edge of the cave. I sighed and stared at the horizon; things were finally coming together. Blanks were filling in and enemies were defined.

"You've got a plan?" I asked.

"Yes. We're going to get the hell out of here. No pun intended," Stranger replied. His voice began to change to almost a growl.

"Are you all right?" I was alarmed at Stranger's sudden change in voice.

"For now, but we've got to hurry."

Stranger spun me around; grabbing onto my torso he expanded his wings and jumped from the cave's ledge. We plummeted into the empty air and Stranger's wings contracted and expanded as we were lifted into the sky.

The wind choked my voice back as we soared through the air.

"Are we going to the seventh pit?"

Stranger simply nodded his head, his gray eyes focused ahead. We flew over the bodies that crawled below us; for miles they stretched. Fire would erupt from the ground now and then and blow a few individuals into the air. A couple of times Stranger had to dodge them.

We just continued to soar over them, their outstretched arms brushing against my body. The tips of their fingers felt like hot strings against my skin.

The sea of bodies extended for miles but came to an abrupt stop unexpectedly. Slowly the mass of bodies became more and more spread out until only a few hundred littered the ground. I looked up at Stranger who had a perplexed look upon his face. Not wanting to bother him with more questions I just allowed him to concentrate.

When we reached a point that revealed deserted ground, Stranger slowed down. Flapping his dark wings a few times, the flight stopped and we slowly lowered to the ground. The rock was hot under my bare feet. Colored an off orange, only prints of hands and feet remained in the sand.

"Stranger, do you see these prints?" I turned to him.

"Yes, what I don't see though is people."

The air was quiet, the type of quiet that caused your toes to curl. With squinted eyes, I looked around, seeing nothing but desert and sand. Worried by the jolted expression on Stranger's face, I ran my fingers through my stringy hair and sighed. "So why did we stop exactly?"

"Something is wrong." Stranger had his fists clenched, which made me nervous.

"Let's just continue. How far are we from—"

Stranger raised his hand to silence me. Almost as if they just materialized from nothing, a line of individuals stood maybe fifty yards away. The lineup of men stretched perhaps a hundred men, all armed with random blunt objects.

"Please tell me those are friends of yours," I said to Stranger.

"Since your disappearance, a lot of people have been looking for you, Slave."

"Those do not look like Cane's men to me," I replied.

"That's because they're not." Stranger stepped forward, his wings tensed up.

It suddenly occurred to me, after looking over the men once more, who they were. Stranger turned his head, penetrating me with his gray eyes.

"They are the Prisoners of Pain," I uttered under my breath.

"That is correct, the one group that loves Lucifer with a passion," Stranger replied.

Filled with a sudden rush of fear, I stepped back a few feet. Stranger cocked his head at me in question." Why are you retreating for a hundred men?"

"Well maybe because there are a hundred of them but only two of us," I replied cynically.

Stranger laughed; his smile radiated from his face. Flexing his wings, he bent his body and sprung from the ground, cracking the stone under his feet. Spiraling into the sky, he roared with fury. The Prisoners of Pain returned the battle cry with a collection of berserker rage.

While Stranger was suspended in the air, the attackers hurled stones and primitive spears at him. Little damage was done; the flint and stones broke at contact with Stranger's husked skin. The hundred men paused for a moment and stared up at Stranger smiling down upon them.

Stranger winked at me, and stunned I watched Stranger's mouth open and a strange golden glow expel from his chomps. Bewitched by the ambient glow, the Prisoners of Pain dropped their remaining weapons and just continued to stare. I took another few steps backwards; I was half bewitched myself. Suddenly an explosion of intense fire erupted from Stranger's jaw; by flapping his wings he directed the flames upon our attackers. The wind caused my eyelids to shutter like a moth's wings. I watched in horror as the flesh of our attackers turned to ash and tumbled off their bones into the wind.

In shock I just stared with my eyes wide open as the hundred men were turned into a hundred skeletons standing at attention. Stranger slowly floated to the ground and touched upon the surface lightly. The bones dropped to the sand shortly afterwards, making the sound of dominos falling.

"Stranger, if we get caught you're going to pay for that," I laughed.

"I'll pay for that big time," Stranger winked at me.

Although we had defeated our opposition, something still did not click. I looked down and ran my feet through the sand, and a thought happened to arise.

"So where did all the people who were here previously go?"

Stranger's smile faded slightly. The thought must have escaped him as well. His eyes seemed to be pointing behind me, so as I turned I stumbled backwards, tripping over my own feet.

Within seconds an attack by thousands was on our backs. Stranger with his eyes wide and anxious grabbed me by my wrist and jumped into the air. He had lifted maybe ten feet into the air when we crashed to the surface once more.

"What happened?" I yelled as the mob jumped onto me.

I heard no reply, and I could not see Stranger through the jumbled heap I was stuck in. Soon I was covered by a blanket of hundreds, imprisoned in darkness once again. Although I could not see the individuals dog piling me, their rotting lips whispered into my ears.

"All of Hell has been searching for you."

"Finally we get some fresh meat!"

"You're going to suffer greatly good-doer."

I shut my eyes, not knowing why I bothered to do so. The voices continued to whisper, going into more of a word salad with no coherence. Slowly the pressure began to relieve off of me, and the orange light sneaked through small cracks of limbs. The last body smothering me finally was thrown off from top of me. My legs had fallen numb, so I could not stand or roll over.

I felt a strong hand clutch the back of my head and pry my face from the sand. The light still blinded me a pinch, and the face was blurry but I recognized it—it was Lacious!

"Well, look at you, Slave! Have you lost weight? You look good," Lacious said, right before he thrust my head into the sand.

Like an ostrich my head was stuck in the sand. Lacious pulled my head from the ground and tossed me a few feet just for a chance to stare me down more. Quickly I looked around me, trying to get an idea of the situation.

Stranger had disappeared, or at least I could not see him. The mass population of disgruntled bodies crawled across the surface once more but tended to stray away from Lacious, giving him a radius within which to maneuver.

I rubbed the back of my head and coughed up a question. "Where is Stranger?"

Lacious puckered his green lips but denied me a reply. I pulled myself to my feet, holding my ribcage which pain was coming back.

"I guess you've learned the truth now?"

"Yes, for the most part," I replied.

Lacious simply raised his arms to the air; at the gesture a soul sucker swept down and landed beside him. The soul sucker's talons dug into a few individuals crawling around, sinking into their backs causing them to cry out in pain.

With a snap of his fingers, Lacious motioned toward me. Knowing I could not win the fight, I submitted and walked toward the soul sucker. I had to cross a small patch of crawlers; it felt like walking during an earthquake. Finally, after reaching Lacious, I mounted the soul sucker.

Lacious mounted the creature's neck, grabbed hold of the reigns, and we soared into the sky. I shut my eyes but reopened them as Lacious grunted in anger.

On our tails was another soul sucker, mounted by Stranger. I smiled at the sight of him but was alarmed by the reason he was not flying himself—the massive feathered wings appeared to have been ripped from his body.

Stranger's soul sucker caught up, neck to neck with ours. Both demons' eyes radiated with demented hatred for each other. Lacious licked his upper lip then hollered a command to Stranger.

"Land at once, that is an order!"

Stranger glared at Lacious, and his smile spread across his face ear to ear. With his fist raised, Stranger flipped the bird to Lacious.

"The deal is off!" Stranger shouted, intimidating with his newly toned voice.

Stranger steered his ride into Lacious'. The collision knocked me from my mount; I went spinning toward the ground below. Lacious flipped his hair back, then stood on his mount growling under his breath. Stranger slowed down his soul sucker by pulling on its reigns, and Lacious leaped at Stranger tackling him from the mount.

The bodies that crawled the surface broke my fall, although I heard a few bones snap at my impact. Shortly after my crash, the two demons cratered into the desert surface. I struggled to my feet and limped off away from the scene.

Lacious and Stranger were locked into each other. It had become a shoving contest, the two demons trying not to trip over the men beneath their feet.

I stopped after a while, turned, and watched Stranger fight Lacious. With my fingers crossed I found myself bouncing and biting my lip in anticipation.

Lacious clutched Stranger by the stubs that were once his wings and twisted onto them. Stranger screamed and retaliated by elbowing Lacious then jumped him, biting into his neck. Blood trickled down Lacious' chest, then Lacious countered by grabbing Stranger by the neck and throwing him into the air like a child.

Stranger landed on an individual's cranium but quickly jumped to his feet. I watched Stranger's posture tense up as he opened his mouth and it began to glow like it had before.

Lacious laughed while stretching out his arm and pointed his finger at Stranger. Stranger's gray eyes began to water and filled with dark tears as he began to gag. He was choking on his own flames.

Fallen to his knees, Stranger held his throat and looked up at Lacious with anxiety. Lacious loomed over him with his hands on his hips.

"Tell me now, did you really think you'd get away with it all?" Lacious asked.

Stranger still choked up, nodded his head with a vague smile. Enraged, Lacious slapped him. The slap echoed and even made my cheek hurt.

"Don't worry; we will break you of your humor before eternity is up." Lacious snapped his fingers and Stranger gasped; the flames released and erupted into the sky.

16. Lucifer's Conquest

Once more I found myself caged like an animal. Lacious had taken us to Lucifer, for what purpose had not been made clear yet. At least my cage was spacious this time, although the bottom of the cage was rusted and cut my feet if I moved too fast. Fifty bars enclosed the cage; trust me, I had counted them a few times.

My little enclosure was bolted to the corner of a throne room, which was decorated with empty frames. In the center of the room was a throne carved from marble. Being carved of marble, it stood out like a sore thumb in a room of oak and cedar.

For the time being I had been left alone, but I suddenly heard approaching footsteps. The heavy tap of feet on tile grew louder until the chamber door opened. Lacious entered the chamber paying me no attention and held the door for Lucifer to follow closely behind.

Lucifer shot me a gaze then walked and sat on his throne. He looked the same as I had remembered; his scaly skin still caused my skin to tingle. With his hands massaging the armrest of his throne, Lucifer's beady little eyes just stared at me.

Lacious leaned in and whispered to Lucifer, and Lucifer beamed up at Lacious with a look of discontent. He then directed his attention back to me.

"Haven't you had some adventure? I have heard you've discovered the identity of Aziel and his origin. I have heard you've learned of my genius plan of conquering Paradise. I have heard you came into contact with Cane and his tribe. Now tell me, is what I have heard true?" Lucifer interlocked his fingers.

I projected my gaze to the floor as I answered. "If what you are asking me is if I've learned my guardian angel sold me out, then yes. If you're trying to learn if I know about what the deal consisted of, then also yes I do. Finally, if you're concerned about Cane, I can assure you he couldn't even get me safely down a stream."

Lacious and Lucifer collectively laughed. Lacious peeled some gunk from the corner of his mouth and spoke.

"We're not concerned about Cane. He is no threat to the Master's plans; we are just trying to assess what's developed since we last saw you."

"You want to know if my memory returned," I answered.

Lucifer was about to speak when the door opened once more. Dressed in a dark tunic, a man entered and approached Lucifer. He had a thick curly beard and eyes of deep sadness. His lips moved; he was about to speak when he caught glimpse of my presence. We made eye contact; his deep brown spheres penetrated me almost as if trying to read my mind. Kneeling against the back of the cage, I furrowed my eyebrows trying to read his facial expression toward me.

"What is it Judas?" Lucifer said, cutting off our staring contest.

Judas tripped over his words a few times, unable to take his eyes off me. Finally though as Lacious stepped toward him, he was able to spit out what he had to say.

"I was just wondering if you needed anything else before I left," Judas meekly answered.

"Yes Judas, fetch me Aziel."

"Yes. Right away—" Judas cut himself off; his gaze was still focused on me as he slipped out the room.

The chamber door shut behind Judas, and we remained exchanging stares until he would return with Stranger. Lucifer and Lacious would share whispers now and then, while I just recounted the number of bars in my cage.

Eventually, Stranger arrived to the room. He wore a black cape, I assumed to hide his mutilated wings. As he entered Lucifer pointed toward the floor. Stranger did not even make eye contact with me; he just dropped to his knees and bowed his head. I could not believe what I was seeing; there was for sure no hope for me now. Lacious looked smugly at me and winked.

"Stranger, what are you doing?" I shouted at him, but he did not respond.

"Sorry Slave, he's been down here too long. There is nothing angelic left in him," Lacious happily said.

Stranger turned his head and gave me a dead stare. He stood to his feet and took the left place of Lucifer. Lacious looked over at him and nodded his head.

"Realize now there remains no hope. The sooner you accept that, the sooner we can continue. When Aziel first came to me with our deal, I offered him a place of power in the universe. I'm willing to do the same for you; all you must do is bow your head to me and help us on our quest," Lucifer said, trying to charm me.

I did not answer him. With crossed arms, I turned my face up and ignored their presence. I knew I would probably regret this eventually, but there was no way I was swearing allegiance to Lucifer.

"Everyone has a breaking point," Lacious directed toward Lucifer.

"Yes, I know. If I can break an angelic protector, I can break this pathetic man in half." Lucifer smirked, then stood to his feet and walked toward the door.

Lacious followed closely behind and opened the door to allow Lucifer to exit. Lacious followed, leaving Stranger standing alone in front of me. I looked at him then smiled; it must have been a trick!

"Great, let me out, Stranger!" I ran toward the front of the cage, waving for him to hurry.

Stranger just stared at me, his eyes completely dead.

"My name is Aziel."

My gut clenched up as I realized it was no trick. With a swoop of his cape, Stranger turned and left the chamber. As the door closed behind him, I was left in solitude to think.

In my daze I was not aware that the chamber door was opened and I was no longer alone. My legs outstretched, I rested my head on the set of bars causing an imprint to appear on my neck. In the shadows though I heard a voice.

"Hello, I want to help you."

I required a few moments to process the voice. Slowly turning my head, I saw the man from earlier squatting in front of my cage. From a closer view, the man named Judas had deep wrinkles in his face, and his throat looked as if it had been strangled.

I got to my feet and looked down at Judas.

"You want to help me? Can you get me out of here?"

Judas did not even waste time to nod his head or reply—he quickly brought out a set of keys from his tunic. Fumbling with the dozen keys that must have been on the ring, he finally managed to get my cage door open.

I had one foot out of the cage before it could even swing completely open. Judas gave me an anxious look as he scurried off in a shuffling manner.

"Follow me, we must hurry!" Judas disappeared from the room and left the door hanging open.

Staying alert, I followed his lead into the hallway. I shut the door as I exited, and I found myself in a long dark hallway. The hall was lighted by small torches every ten feet, and a red carpet ran down the center of the hall. I looked down both ends, trying to decide which way Judas most likely went. As I was about to take the left route, Judas appeared from the shadows of the right.

"Quickly, let us go this way. We really must hurry, we can't waste any time." Judas motioned for me to follow as once again he shuffled off.

His feet barely lifted off the ground as he ran; I followed him until we reached the end of the hall. Judas took a sharp right onto a staircase, so I followed.

"Where are we going?" I tried to ask.

Judas waved his hand in dismissal as he led me down the stairway. As we finally reached ground level, I ran with him toward what appeared to be an old carriage.

"Run for the wagon!" Judas urged me as he picked up his pace.

I had reached the carriage when I heard an animal's roar from the distance. Climbing into the carriage, I poked my head out from a burgundy curtain of the carriage's cab. The building I had just escaped was a titanic castle; Lacious stood at the top tower with his hair flying in the wind.

"Judas, you traitor, you will pay dearly!" Lacious screamed.

I glanced at Judas who stared into thin air dazed, and I cocked my head. "Perhaps we should go," I said cynically.

Judas snapped out of whatever trance he was in and jumped out of the wagon to climb into the driver's seat. With a grip on the reigns, two old stallions exploded into a full-out gallop. I looked out the back window of the carriage to see Stranger standing next to Lacious on the castle tower.

Having reached a considerably safe distance, I took the time to take in my new predicament. The carriage was not in rotting condition, and the stallions allowing us to escape looked healthy. My first guess was that Judas stole this carriage from Lucifer. Soft red fabric draped the doors and covered the seats; a small window in the front of the carriage allowed the passenger to talk to the driver.

Jumping to the opposite seat, I leaned in the window. "Thanks, by the way."

"What?" Judas leaned back, the gallop of the horses deafening my voice.

"I said thanks."

"I can't hear you; we're almost there though."

About to ask where, the scenery around me gained my attention. The carriage was running across a stone bridge and molten lava rushed underneath. My jaw dropped in awe, at first at the sight of the molten substance but then at the giant campsite I saw we were heading toward.

The carriage came to a stop in front of a small tattered tent. Stepping outside, I viewed hundreds of tents pitched up. Men circled campfires and grouped logs into stockpiles. Judas jumped from the driver's seat and shuffled over to me.

"What were you saying earlier?"

Still awestruck by the situation, I answered sheepishly, "Thanks."

"Oh, well no problem. Will you follow me now?"

With a nod of my head, I followed Judas through a labyrinth of tents and conversing individuals. We arrived at the centerpoint of the campsite. At the centerpoint was built a larger square tent. It was colored green, but a tan blanket was used as a door. Judas stopped at the entrance and motioned with his eyes for me to follow him.

Entering the main tent, I looked around to see if I could find anything interesting. Except for the crude charcoal drawings on the tent's walls, the inside was completely unfurnished and empty. Judas stood at the center of the tent and smiled at me.

"I'm so glad you're here." He nervously rubbed his hands together.

"That's nice, Judas. Now can you tell me what is going on?"

Judas rolled his eyes in circles as he sighed. "We know about you; we know what you're being forced to do."

"I guess that's common knowledge down here by now. That doesn't explain these hundreds of individuals or you busting me out earlier," I replied.

"Do you know how I ended up here?" Judas's eyes were focused on my forehead.

I cleared my throat and lifted my heavy gaze from Judas.

"Yes. You betrayed. . . ."

Judas's lip began to tremble, tears enveloped his eyes. He fell to the ground, his knees giving out on him. With his arms thrown in the air, he let out a cry. I felt sorry for him and ran over and placed my palm on his shoulder. Wiping tears from his eyes, he looked up at me.

"I don't know why I did it. I was pressured; I didn't think they would kill him! They said they only wanted to question him!" Judas cried.

"You're not the first, and not the last, to make decisions that lead to damnation." I did not think that was very soothing, but it was the only thing I could think to say.

Judas collected himself. "I don't want to spend eternity down here. I've suffered so much!"

Not wanting to say any more, I patted his back. "Who are all these people?"

"The Bellowing Bystanders, many of these men and women made a lot of mistakes in life. Some weren't raised in a household that believed in faith, and because of that they grew to be damned," Judas said, as he got back to his feet.

"We had learned about Aziel and his deal with Lucifer, and a lot of us became afraid. If Lucifer were to gain that kind of power, to control Paradise, not a thing in the universe would be safe," Judas continued.

"So what do you want me to do?" I asked.

"Many of us thought if we were to stop Lucifer from succeeding, then perhaps God will forgive us. He might offer us salvation!" The look on Judas's face brightened up at the idea of Paradise.

Judas reached out and held me by my wrist. "Will you please help us?"

I had little choice; there was no way I was going to spend eternity in Hell. I might as well have an army backing me up.

"Yes," I replied to him.

Judas jumped to his feet, and his face beamed with excitement. "This is great, I'll tell the men."

Watching him shuffle out of the tent, I took the time to let everything soak in. I breathed in and out with nice long breaths. Finally after I felt calmed down I exited the tent to find hundreds of men circling me. Judas stood in the circle in front of me with a grimace on his face.

Feeling scared I backed up a few feet as the army of Bellowing Bystanders threw their arms into the air with a battle cry. Although I was afraid at first, I soon realized they were throwing their arms up for me.

With my eyes widened, I looked upon the men and realized I now had my own army.

17. Alliance with Cane

"I would like to introduce you to the top men of our faction. They all wanted to speak with you; they have some theories on how we can achieve success." Judas stood in front of me, a group of men behind him.

The Bellowing Bystanders had made me the commander of their army. Taking advantage of the situation, I had requested the center tent to be furnished with my own chair and other items of my choice. Most of the furniture I had been brought had been fashioned together by rotten wood and rusty nails. I had to be careful when sitting on my chair; a large nail protruded from the bottom and looked potentially painful.

Judas had brought four men before me. They lined the back of the tent wall, partially hidden by shadows. I could make the first figure out to look Persian in features, and he wore tarnished battle armor. The second man was very short, coming only to the other man's waistline. The second individual also wore a funny hat, which I had to bite my tongue not to laugh at. The third and fourth men were too hidden by shadows even to make out at all.

"All right Judas, what are their ideas?" I said, not exactly knowing how a commander was supposed to talk.

Judas shuffled his feet to the men and spoke to the Persian. With a nod of his head, the Persian stepped forward into the light. He had short hair and spoke with an accent.

"You had an idea?" I asked the man.

Speaking with his hands, the Persian began to speak to me. "Yes, I suggest we round our forces up and attack from behind. Lucifer and his forces would not expect such a move."

I pretended to think it was a good idea, although in reality I imagined it to be stupid. That kind of attack had been done so often in history there was no way Lucifer would not see that coming.

Judas shook the Persian's hand before he went back into formation. Judas then motioned for the next man to step forward and speak, but turning to the line he realized he was missing.

"Oh, where did he go?" Judas asked before the short man tugged on his tunic. Looking down, Judas saw the tiny man. "There you are."

"Shut up, Judas," the short man said with a French accent.

I was amused at the facial expression Judas shot me as a result of the harsh words issued toward him. Trying to think of what a man of my position would do, I motioned with my hands for them to move on.

Stepping farther up than the Persian, almost as if to prove he was better, the short man spoke to me.

"I am Napoleone Buonaparte. Although amused at a straightforward attack on Lucifer, I think we should choose another method."

"What would that be, Napoleone?" Judas snapped at him.

Napoleone waved off Judas's remark and continued. "Lucifer's forces are still too great for us to overcome. Why not strengthen our numbers?"

Interested in the idea Napoleone was presenting, I asked for him to expand. "Who could we get to join us?"

The Persian took the occasion to step up once again. "He's speaking of the Tribe of Cane."

"Was somebody speaking to you?" Napoleone threw his hat to the ground and jumped on it.

Judas quickly shuffled in between the men. The idea of getting Cane to help us seemed beneficial in theory. I mean, for one thing I had no idea how to lead an army. An army was what it was going to take to get out of Hell without being stopped though.

"Do you think Cane would join forces?" I asked.

The two men still were bickering; Judas was having difficulties keeping the two apart.

"I said, do you think it's really possible?"

Now the two other men had joined the brawl. Judas hollered in Latin as he was pinned between the four brutes, and the tent was drowned by the sound of grunting, slapping, and the hard snap of fists against skin.

Tired of trying to get order, I stood from my chair and walked around the dog fight. I exited the tent without being seen. As I leaned against a wooden post outside, eventually Judas stepped out from the tent. He had two black eyes, his lip had been busted, and a trail of blood went down his neck. He slowly limped over to me and placed his hand on my shoulder. "That went very well."

The comfortable feeling of being backed by an entire army had grown less after that little show. Although I felt I had finally made some progress anyway.

Soon we had the camp torn down, and we began our voyage to the lower sixth. Judas walked beside me, mostly since I had no idea where we were headed. Our caravan of Bellowing Bystanders stretched for miles like a giant caterpillar.

"How are you doing?" Judas leaned in.

I fashioned the best look of confidence I could muster but finally replied truthfully, "Even with hundreds of men behind me, I still feel vulnerable."

Judas smiled. "That is understandable. You would have to be a fool not to feel that way. I just hope we stand a chance."

"We should be looking at the bright side, shouldn't we?" I joked.

With a chuckle Judas replied, "Unfortunately Hell is not a good atmosphere for optimism."

After an exchange of mutual agreement I felt as if I should change the subject. We had traveled a great distance already; soon we would be reaching the lower sixth.

"In what section are your four strongest men Judas?" I asked.

Judas shot me a worried glance.

"What is it?" I questioned again.

Wiping sweat from his brow, Judas shrugged his shoulders. "Napoleone is leading the center faction; the two you were not able to meet are in the rear."

"What about the Persian?"

"Did you say the Persian?" Judas repeated.

"Yes, the Persian."

"Well, he did not agree with our plan," Judas finally spit out.

"Didn't agree? So he stayed behind?" I asked.

"Not exactly; he took some of our men and went with his own plan of attacking from behind." Judas finally sighed once it was out and gave me a big uncomfortable smile.

I stopped to think. Looking at the ground, I could see Judas's dirty tunic drag against the dirt; the unorganized marching behind me kept me from clearing my mind.

"This is bad. I don't know much about commanding, but you would think if the Persian attacks before we even get a chance to meet with Cane, our entire element of surprise would be lost."

"Well yes," Judas agreed as we continued to walk.

We did not continue our conversation but just kept up our march. One of the men from behind us finally yelled that we were approaching some people on the road ahead of us.

"Who are those giants?" I heard Judas say before I could even see the men blocking our path.

The four giants before us were none other than the four barbarians I had met earlier on my journey. I elbowed Judas in the rib, giving him a wink.

"Don't worry, I know these men."

"Good, you can go talk with them." Judas said anxiously.

With a light laugh I began to walk toward the four barbarians. They at first did not recognize me, but soon after, cocking their heads, they all beamed smiles.

"Well look at this lad. We thought you would be in Lucifer's hands by now!" Ivan bellowed.

"It is a long story. We need to see Cane," I told Victor.

"Now there's a we?" Victor said as he looked over my shoulder at the mass of men.

"I think we can help each other," I replied, taking back Victor's attention.

"You can come speak with Cane, lad, but we can't allow an entire army of men to enter the village."

I clenched my fist slightly. I did not know how safe I would be going back to see Cane alone.

"I want to bring one other man with me," I said.

Horace and Victor nodded and turned back toward the village. I ran over to Judas; my limp had finally gotten better.

"They are going to take me and you back to Cane."

"Leave our men?" Judas said tensely.

"Don't worry, it won't take long; we'll be in and out," I assured him.

Judas and I followed the barbarians back to the village. We had to travel in a small canoe for half the trip. Once again I found myself squashed between the four brutes, but this time at least I had some company.

The boat reached the banks of Cane, and Horace jumped out of the boat, accidentally nailing me in the jaw with his boot. My vision went spotty for a few seconds as Horace laughed while helping me from the boat.

Shaun and Ivan did not bother with any of us and simply strolled into the village, I assumed to play another round of throw pig. Horace tied up the canoe while Victor led us into Cane's hut.

Pushing past the musty old cloth, it swung into Judas's face, overwhelming him with stench. Squeezing tightly onto his nose, his cheeks turned a reddish shade as we entered and stood against the hut's wall.

Cane sat naked on a bed of hay, the woman without eyelids used a damp rag to wash his body.

"Hello Aziel, I heard you—"

I cut Cane off quickly, wanting to set him straight. "You were wrong."

Cane looked alarmed. He grabbed his partner's wrist, which stopped her from bathing him any further. "Excuse me?"

"You were wrong, Cane. My name is not Aziel. That was my guardian; he was the one who made a deal with the devil, and he sold me out," I informed Cane.

Cane's face turned red, matching Judas's as he still pinched his nose together. After some awkward silence, Cane spoke once more. "It does not matter; the outcome was going to be the same. Who did you bring with you?"

"This is Judas," I replied.

Cane smiled devilishly. He signaled for his woman to continue bathing him. The dirty water rolled down his body, spilling onto the ground, soaking the dirt and making it mud.

"Judas got me out of Lucifer's capture," I let Cane know.

"That's impressive. I'd think it would be quite difficult for somebody to get such a valuable item away from Lucifer. I'd think it would be closely guarded," Cane taunted.

"What are you trying to say?" Judas said with edge.

"Weren't you the traitor of man?" Cane continued.

Judas looked as if he were about to pounce. I quickly got in the middle.

"Judas wishes to earn salvation; he has an army ready to join you."

"Join him? He can join us!" Judas yelled before ranting in Latin.

"Either way, whomever joins whoever, what are you planning on doing? Defeating Lucifer? Killing him?" Cane laughed; Horace and Victor joined in, covering their laughs with their palms, but their jiggling bellies could not hide the laughter fully.

Judas, disgusted at the conversation, stormed outside. I remained where I stood because I knew we needed Cane's help.

"Well, what was your plan?"

"It is different than your friend's there. Our plan was to conquer Paradise for ourselves; in fact we still can, now that you've returned."

"Before you think of doing anything, how would you plan on conquering Paradise? You think you can defeat you-know-who?" I asked.

A sober look came upon Cane's face. Finally, after closing his eyes tightly, he opened them and replied, "It's better trying than rotting down here."

I smiled at Cane and took a couple steps forward. "Help us, Cane. Join us, and maybe we can all get out of here and earn a spot in Paradise."

Cane agreed to join our cause and left with me outside the hut. Judas paced the beach, and as he saw us come out he shuffled toward us tensely.

"He's with us, Judas," I assured him, feeling tension between him and Cane.

Judas kept his eyes on Cane when he replied, "We should head back then. I left Napoleone in charge until we would return."

"All right, let's go."

Cane turned to Horace and Victor. "Go round everyone up. Tell them we're finally moving in on the seventh pit. You should get there before we do most likely."

Horace laughed, slapped Victor on the back, and left. They had a bounce in their step; I assumed they were finally excited to get some action. Cane turned back to me. "All right let's go."

Judas and I huddled into Cane's boat once more; Cane, almost in a gallop, untied the small vessel and grabbed his oar before pushing the boat into the water. I stared up at the sky; the clouds were at a standstill and practically had disappeared.

For the remainder of the ride down the stream, nobody spoke to one another. Solemn looks were exchanged between the three of us till we reached the end of the stream. Cane craned his neck around, looking at barren land.

"Where are these men you were speaking about?" Cane asked.

I had slipped into a daze but snapped out of it and looked around. I could not see a single man. Judas also looked alarmed; he half stood up and looked back and forth similar to a how a squirrel would behave.

"I hope this isn't another setup," Cane growled.

"No, it is no setup," Judas snorted, attracting our gazes.

The boat floated against the bank, bobbing slightly at the small tides.

"Where is everyone, Judas?" I asked in a worried tone.

"It was Napoleone; I can't stand that man," Judas released with retired breath.

"What's he mean, Napoleone?" Cane asked me.

Judas ran his fingers through his hair. "That short little narcissist; if I had to guess, he ran off with our men."

"Why would he do that?" My bones began to ache.

"Power hungry would be my guess; I always thought he resented not being in command."

Cane begin to snicker; he covered his mouth with his bloodstained hands. Judas thinned his eyelids and sneered at him. "What is funny?"

"You would think out of all people you'd be able to see betrayal coming," Cane retorted with a sarcastic tone.

Judas exploded in rage; he lunged across the boat, tackling Cane. Cane gripped his hands around Judas's throat. The two men strangled each other, and the struggle nearly caused the boat to overturn.

I grabbed Judas by the hair and yanked him away from Cane. I pressed my foot against Cane's throat, attempting to keep the two men apart.

"Stop it! We won't get anywhere fighting."

Cane dropped his arms to his side, and Judas finally relaxed. I released my grip from the two men, and jumped out of the boat. Hitting the sand with a slap, I walked up onto the land with my hands at my side.

Judas stumbled out from the boat, tripped over his own feet, and landed face first in the wet sand. Climbing to his feet, he shuffled over to me. I looked at Judas; his tunic had grown dirtier, sand clung to the garments, and his eyes were filled with anxiety.

"You two need to get along," I told him under my breath.

"I am sorry, but everything is falling apart."

"So fighting amongst each other is going to remedy it?" I said with anger, pointing at the boat. Cane sat, resting his chin in his hand.

Judas stared at the wet sand. A cold breeze brushed against my naked body while I rubbed some grime out of my eye sockets. Cane eventually climbed out from the boat and approached us.

"I couldn't hear you from over there, but I think I know what you were saying."

The three of us shared some silence till Judas finally spoke. "Well, what now?"

"We can meet up with my people. We still have a chance to do this," Cane answered.

We would be following Cane's command if we joined with his men. With Napoleone having control of the Bellowing Bystanders, I guessed this would be the best route for now.

18. Betrayal

Dry wind pressed against us; for miles we traveled, our lips tightly squeezed so blowing sand would not enter them. Cane held his arms close to his chest, his hair flying in front of his face. Judas's beard uncurled in the wind, his tunic pressed against his body like a mold of clay, and I walked behind them both, bent forward fighting the breeze.

The gray sky lowered, which created a fog we lost ourselves in. We followed the stream east under Cane's assurance we would intercept his men.

Eventually when our knees rattled and pebbles collected into our feet, we decided to set up camp until the wind died down. We found refuge from the intense wind behind a giant boulder. The three of us huddled together; all of our teeth shook and rattled.

"We should be running into the men soon," Cane said to us.

"What? You've got to speak louder," Judas replied as the wind whistled through our ears.

"I said we should be with the group soon. Once this wind dies down, it should not take much longer."

I rubbed my hands together in an attempt to create kinetic heat. While I rested my head against the stone surface of the rock, Cane leaned in. "By the way, I'm sorry about the name thing."

I looked at Cane and half smiled. "It's all right."

"May I ask how you found out my error?"

"Stranger, I mean Aziel, was the one who abducted me from Horace and the others. When explaining to him what I had learned, he corrected me, telling me the actuality," I answered.

Judas interrupted our conversation. "Did you ask him what your name is?"

Cane widened his eyes, apparently eager to know if I had as well.

"No, I guess I didn't even think to ask. He did admit to erasing my memory though."

Cane snickered. "Judas and I have seriously sinned in our time, but I can't imagine my own guardian selling me out. You know, if Aziel erased your memory, he could probably restore it," Cane brought up.

I turned to him; I had not thought of that before. "If that were so, he would have done that by now, I'd think."

"Perhaps he has more planned than you think," Judas said with a prophetic tone.

With that our conversation ended. We sat there until the wind eased up, then continued our journey. Mile after mile we kept going till we reached our destination. Over the horizon, we could see Cane's men setting up camp.

"There they are," Cane said, his chest filled with pride.

Judas and I followed Cane; every man we passed issued a salutation to Cane but their eyes strayed from us. Through the camp we went; Cane stopped at a few tents to whisper to a few of his men before he continued to lead us toward the center of the grounds.

I felt perfectly relaxed until I caught a glimpse inside a passing tent. Inside I saw a dozen men hog tied and gagged. The next tent I passed had the same. I made an effort to peek into each tent I passed; I found every one of them to be full of prisoners.

My gut reaction was to hightail it out of there, but I knew I had to play it cool. Judas had not noticed the contents of the hundreds of tents yet, and I figured it would be best he not. I decided to keep my knowledge a secret, until I heard Judas holler out, "It's Napoleone!"

Tied to a stake in the center of the camp was little Napoleone. Shaun stood next to the beam, wearing Napoleone's funny little hat. Napoleone did not look to be in good shape; his uniform had become tatters of fabric, and his right eye swelled up resembling an avocado. He was strapped to the large stake with leather straps, one around his chest, the other his hips. Shaun stood guard, smirking at Judas and me.

Cane stood in front of us, his back turned. He slowly spun around, an evil grin on his face. Judas shuffled back a few steps.

"Why don't I like this, Cane?" I said.

"Did you really think I was going to allow a plan eternity in the making to go to ruins? I apologize for the confusion; your little friend here with the forced French accent did not throw a rebellion. I sent Horace and Victor to do a quick job before you reached them with me. Ivan, please take hold of our friend here."

Ivan stepped forward from the crowd that had gathered and grabbed me by my neck, making sure not to let me use my forehead. Victor then stepped up and bounded me with leather straps. Lifted from the ground, I was bound to the stake, back to back with Napoleone. My face became flushed with panic; I looked at Judas and knew what he was in for.

"Judas, run now!" I urged him.

Judas shuffled backwards, shooting glances at the barbarians. They closed in around him, but just as they were in reaching distance, they all began to laugh. I looked at them confused, not knowing what was going on. Cane turned to me, beaming with glee. He proceeded to walk over to Judas and shake his hand.

"Good job, Judas," Cane said, his eyes still on me.

"Thank you, Cane, it went as smoothly as you said it would."

Were my eyes deceiving me? Judas had manipulated me; I felt so betrayed. Evil grins were smeared across the crowd that watched me like cannibals. Cane began to pace around me.

"Did you think I was not prepared? I have been planning my escape of this dreadful place since I first stepped foot on its first flaming coal. I've got alliances in places you couldn't imagine—how else do you think you would have been rescued so easily? Rest easy, Slave, for soon you'll live true to your name," Cane whispered against my cheek.

Judas and Cane left me; they disappeared into the camp, as did everyone else. I was left alone, with only Napoleone strapped to the stake with me. I attempted to look at him, but the angle was impossible.

"So what happened?" I asked.

"What do you think?" Napoleone snapped.

I sighed and looked up at the sky; the clouds were once again still.

"We were growing impatient. Our impatience made us vulnerable," Napoleone finally spit out.

"That's makes sense; I guess we all screwed up," I replied.

"Understandable is not acceptable. I have invaded countries, led armies, but was fooled by those ape barbarians. I cannot believe Judas sold out his own men."

I had to smile at that remark. "I really thought he wanted redemption."

Napoleone spit to the ground. "Learn this fast: very few men will pass a chance for revenge for redemption."

This was very true.

"All right, so let's size things up. Judas sold us out and is now sided with Cane. Cane has hundreds of men armed and ready with hundreds of others tied up; he could probably get them to join him as well easily, and we are tied to a pole. Our odds are looking pretty bad."

"Don't be ridiculous," Napoleone chuckled.

"What? Sure, I would think Lucifer would always have an upper hand, but so far Canes been winning this war. Now he has me and Lucifer doesn't."

"You either overestimate Cane, or underestimate Lucifer."

"Do you know something, which I don't?" I asked.

"What do you know in the first place?" Napoleone snorted.

He was right; so far I'd been clueless about everything. I was silent; I waited for Napoleone to continue.

"Lucifer has more control over the situation than you think. My guess would be he knows exactly what is going on and exactly where you are. He's simply weeding out his challengers, if you can call them that. Also, if it even matters, I have heard wind about Lacious sending some German out to fetch the famous Jack the Ripper."

"Well, that meeting didn't turn out very well," I laughed.

"What makes you say that?"

"I just have a hunch. I don't think they were talking the same language." I found it quite funny, but Napoleone was not amused.

Napoleone's silence was a sign to me the conversation had ended. In the distance I could hear the squeal of a pig and broken wood.

My body was worn out; I looked up at the sky as the clouds moved again. The shapes of the clouds relaxed me, so I was surprised to look down and see Napoleone gawking up at me. My mouth moved but no words came out.

"Don't ask," Napoleone uttered as he jumped up and gnawed at my leather straps.

After a chipped tooth, he had gotten me out of bondage. I fell to the ground, my knees shaking. I looked down at Napoleone and half grinned.

"Follow me," Napoleone commanded as he scurried toward a large tent.

I ducked low and followed him. We peeked inside of every tent, finding nothing but tied up Bystanders. I attempted to untie them, but Napoleone assured me it be best to leave them be for now. After hard consideration I agreed with him, and we kept moving.

Finally we had reached our destination. Napoleone picked up a sharp rock and cut a peephole into the large tan tent. He followed by cutting a second hole for me, and we both peeked into the tent where a meeting was going on.

Cane stood at the back of the tent, the four barbarians behind him. Judas sat cross-legged to his left, and a group of Cane's fighters crowded around.

Cane raised his bloodied hands and addressed his men.

"I am aware of all your concerns. You know, however, the amount of time and consideration I've put into this plan. I've stood here and listened to all of you, and now allow me to reply.

"Jacob, you ask how we expect to get past Lucifer's defenders. We have the ultimate bargaining chip. We have plenty of men to decoy our main efforts, and once we get Slave through the gate, we're home free.

"You are all aware of the incarnate variable. If an individual is damned and their body is destroyed, since one cannot perish after death, their bodies are reestablished at Hell's entrance. The determining difference between a damned soul and the soul of someone as Slave that is Slave is marked as saved. Lucifer will not remain in custody of him."

Napoleone and I kept watching through our peepholes as one of the villagers spoke out. "So if all that needs to be done is to kill Slave, then why don't we just burn his body? He'd be reestablished at Heaven's gate since he's saved."

Cane signed and threw up his arms. "Your idea has two holes. For one, by doing that we would give Lucifer just as much chance to attack as we would. Second, Slave has no memory of who he is. Don't give me that look; you should all know he would have to say his name in order to open the gates to Paradise."

The tent became silent. Finally somebody stood to speak. "So what do we do?"

"We need to find Aziel; he's the only one who can give him his name. So, as long as you keep Lucifer occupied, I have something planned that will change the cosmos."

The crowd of fighters all exploded with applause and whistles. I went to tap Napoleone on the shoulder but just fingered air. I took my eye off the peephole to see Napoleone missing. To my left I heard a noise; quickly I looked up at the left—a large tear was cut into the tent, and I heard screaming inside. Napoleone went in for an attack.

That crazy little guy had no chance against a room full of men twice his size. I felt as if I should help, but knowing the odds, I ran off to escape.

19. Caleb

My mouth was parched. With no idea how many miles I walked, I feared if I did not continue they would catch up with me. Defining them, although, had become quite difficult. Every alliance I'd seemed to find had so far turned out to betray me or sell me out. I guessed that was what you would expect out of social settings in Hell.

I was no longer in the cooler, stale climate of Cane's land. The sky was a peel of orange, and the heat rose from the sand, visible like steam. I trudged along though, knowing I could not stop.

At the sight of a large flat stone, I ran to it and took a seat. The smooth surface of the stone was cold, and for the first time in miles I could take a load off. The sand was so hot, flesh peeled from my bone; I would not dare take a seat on such hot surface.

I leaned over and pressed my cheek on the cold smoothness of the flat stone. I could not believe it was so refreshing in this hot atmosphere. I closed my eyes to enjoy the coolness when I heard a voice.

"It feels nice doesn't it?"

I shot up and looked around to see who was talking. I could not see anybody. At the sound of a hiss, I looked to my right and saw a long serpent sitting next to me. Its head arched up at me, and a long, skinny tongue flicked in and out.

"How does it feel?

I jumped to the hot sand in shock; a serpent was actually talking. Steam rose from between my toes as the serpent shook its body.

"Please, return to the stone; that sand looks so painful."

Slowly, I paced back to the stone and hopped onto the cool surface. I kept a safe distance the entire time.

"Did you just talk?"

The serpent coiled up, resting his small head on its body.

"Yes, I could see you were tired. Your lips appear to be chapped as well. How'd you enjoy a nice glass of water?"

I stared at the serpent; I did not trust it at all. It hissed, amused at itself.

"Do you realize the power you possess? You have all of Hell wanting you in their clutches. Don't be fooled, though, there are many sides to this dice."

"So where does a talking serpent fit in?" I asked sarcastically.

The serpent uncoiled itself, then slithered up my arm and whispered into my ear, "My name is Gadrel."

Gadrel's name tickled my ear, at which I quickly grabbed the serpent and threw him onto the desert sand. The serpent hissed loudly as steam rose from its body. The serpent's body began to contort, the scales expanded, and the long slim body of the serpent began to transform. I looked in horror as, from the serpent's destroyed body, a being emerged. With a light gook covering its body, a man with flawless skin rose from the ground, feathered wings slowly erected from his back. A charming face looked up at me. The man appeared to be an angel; he had sparkling blue eyes and blond hair that waved in the wind. The only different features were the two white horns that were on his forehead.

I just sat on my stone with a dead stare at Gadrel. Gadrel wiggled his tongue out before he crept up to me, his feet sizzling under the sand. He plumped onto a seat next to me with a grin on his face.

"What do you want? No more games," I said under my breath.

Gadrel put his arm around me; his skin was hot and caused me to itch.

"There is a lot you don't know."

I simply nodded.

"Some things perhaps it's best you don't know. Although I do have something you might be interested in." Gadrel snickered as he presented me with an apple.

The apple caught my attention; it was the brightest apple I'd ever seen, and it almost glowed. I moved my attention to Gadrel's eyes; I could see my own sad reflection in his blue spheres.

"I don't get it."

"You will soon. Eat this, it will give you knowledge," Gadrel replied.

Slowly I took the apple from Gadrel's palm. I could see myself in the apple, but it was not the sad reflection from Gadrel's eyes. This vision of me was magnificent; I looked incredible. I glanced at Gadrel, who was nodding his head, his arm still around me. I was overcome with a sense of hunger I had missed for a long while; I bit into the apple and slowly chewed. My eyes closed and I became rushed with memories; the apple dropped from my hand, hit the steaming sand, and was instantly cooked. Gadrel's eyes were wide, and his mouth expanded with laughter.

Gadrel removed his arm from behind me; as a result I fell backwards, hitting my head on the flat stone. I could see the sky swirling around me, the orange climaxing into different hues. I saw Gadrel in the air hovering over me.

A stinging sensation exploded in my head as I became overloaded with memories and thoughts. My body went into seizures and convulsed. Gadrel just stared down at me as I shook uncontrollably. Then suddenly my body shot into an arch and, with one final jolt, crashed to the stone's surface. I felt no energy at all; I could not move a single limb, and all I could do was release a single whisper. "My name is Caleb."

With that, my body went completely numb. Gadrel lowered himself onto the stone and stood over me. He bent down and lifted me up. With a silent expression he ascended into the air and through the clouds.

Gadrel's laugh penetrated my skull, even though his mouth did not even move. We pierced the sky, and his wings sliced through the dirty clouds as if they were merely butter. Paralyzed, I could only watch defenselessly as I was swept across a barren land miles above the ground.

Gadrel reached his destination point once a castle came along the horizon. It appeared to be the same castle I had escaped earlier. He circled the titanic structure a few laps, which gave me time to look upon it with my motionless eyes.

The stones of the castle were in their own right enormous, looking to weigh at least a ton each. A tower was built on all four corners, and a depressing moan seemed to escape from the mortar it was kept together with.

Gadrel must have reached a decision; he perched upon the northeast tower and dropped me to the brick flooring. Having felt a pain on impact, I knew feeling was slowly returning to my body. Gadrel jumped from his perch, landing with a foot on either side of my body.

I heard footsteps approach but was still not able to move my eyes. Gadrel moved his gaze from down at me to the second guest who had just joined us. The second individual showed himself after he loomed over at me. The face I looked upon was that of Lacious.

"What did you do to him, Gadrel?" Lacious shot a glance at the other demon.

"Nothing Lacious, I just fetched him as you asked of me." Gadrel had a sinister grin on his face.

Lacious thinned his eyes, and curled his lips. "You did not do what I think you did, did you?"

"You wanted his memory to return, did you not?" Gadrel replied.

"He could have swallowed a seed, you fool!" Lacious yelled as yellow spit splattered from his mouth.

Gadrel chuckled. Lacious bent down, his hair fell on me tickling my face.

"We could have had Aziel return his memory. I don't know what you're planning, Gadrel, but don't let Lucifer know you gave him that apple."

"Don't worry; he'll be back to normal in no time." Gadrel leaned over and patted my stomach.

"You and your damn fruit, Gadrel! Now I'll have to cover up this mess. For your own sake, I hope you're not up to something, Gadrel."

"Of course not; when am I ever up to something?" Gadrel replied as he stepped onto the tower's ledge and leaped off, soaring into the sky.

Lacious slapped my cheek a few times; the feeling had returned to my fingers. Eventually my body returned to normal, but my head still rung, filled with new memories.

Lacious escorted me to a chamber deep in the castle. The chamber he had brought me was colored midnight blue, and frescoes were painted on the ceiling.

Lacious sat me in the corner of the room; I rested my limbs, slowly building my strength back. I watched for the first time as Lacious paced the room nervously.

I rubbed my forehead; the carved digits throbbed against my hand. Whatever that apple was Gadrel gave me, it resulted in me now knowing who I was. My name was Caleb Stone; I lived in a small town inside Ohio. I had written for a local newspaper for most of my adult life. I could remember small parts of a childhood; I saw glimpses of Christmas and Halloween.

I squeezed my eyes and concentrated hard to remember more. My thoughts went to an image of a woman, but before I could explore it I was slapped by Lacious.

"Stop daydreaming, Slave!" Lacious ordered.

My jaw stung as if it had been hit by a boulder, but I slowly turned my head back to Lacious. Aziel now stood at the doorway.

"Gadrel gave him the fruit of knowledge?" Aziel's tone was flat and empty.

Lacious sighed and turned around to face Aziel. "Yes, but we need to say you returned his memory."

"So he remembers his name?"

Lacious glanced at me and nodded his head. His hair bounced and fell upon his shoulders tensely.

Aziel turned his eyes from Lacious to me, as he asked his next question. "Does he remember his death?"

I did remember my death; my mouth opened to tell Aziel what I was thinking, but Lacious cut me off. "That is trivial right now, Aziel," Lacious snarled.

Aziel whipped around and his dark cape created a breeze that blew my strands of hair back. While he studied one of the demonic frescos, Lacious continued to rant.

"Gadrel is also trivial at this point. He's always had a knack for complicating things, which is not news. Everything is lined up as planned. Lucifer is ready to move, but if he were to learn about Gadrel's little stunt, it could mean very bad things for both of us."

Aziel sighed and turned to face Lacious. "I understand; I will go along with your cover story. Now will you leave us?"

"Excuse me?" Lacious snapped.

"I agreed to follow your story; now leave the chamber before I change my mind."

Lacious shot Aziel a look of resentment as he exited the chamber, the chamber door slammed behind him. Aziel's red skin looked almost black under the room's wall color. He set his eyes upon me, while he slowly paced closer toward me.

"I've never seen Lacious so worked up," I softly said.

"A lot is on the line, Caleb." Aziel's eyes rested on me.

I could not help but smile at my journey's progression. I remembered the first pit; I was a nameless slave digging holes. Aziel was a charming stranger who fell into my suffering. Things had changed greatly since then.

"What is with the need for a cover story?" I asked, not knowing my boundaries with Aziel now that he had completely turned.

"That is of no consequence to you right now. What you should concern yourself with, Caleb, is what will transpire very soon," Aziel coldly said.

"Lucifer wants me to open the gate to Paradise," I whispered, almost as if I were speaking blasphemy.

Aziel knelt down to one knee and looked at me at eye level. He massaged his chin, almost as if choosing the proper words to say. "You're going to be sacrificed."

"I don't understand any of this," I replied.

"That's the beauty of it, Caleb; you don't need to. Soon Lucifer will use you to gain entrance once more into Paradise."

I grinded my teeth together as my forehead throbbed.

"Tell me at least one thing. Once I'm sent to Paradise, what makes you think I'll hold the doors for you all?" I said, feeling triumphant.

Aziel gave me a half grin and leaned in close, almost kissing distance, opened his mouth, and whispered, "I'll be with you."

Speechless, I just sat in the corner and watched Aziel stand up and walk out of the room. His cape flew behind him as if being carried by invisible serfs.

20. Attack on Lucifer

The frescoes that covered the ceilings were really remarkable. Hundreds of images decorated the plaster ceiling; many depicted a battle between angels. I strolled along the edge of the room, processing image by image until I had found I had looked at every fresco in the room.

The numbness in my body had passed; I could now feel the cold marble floor under my feet. The marble was black with white swirls, and the frescoes from the ceiling reflected on it, almost in a mirror-like illusion.

Frustrated, I did not feel like just sitting and accepting defeat. Having received the revelation of my identity, I felt a renewed hope. Perhaps I could escape this damned place after all.

My attention eventually went to the only door in the room. It was a solid door, strange carvings decorated it, and light from the torches outside snuck in from the crevice at the bottom of the door. Slowly I walked over to the door and pressed my ear against it.

Not hearing a soul, I placed my hand cautiously around the doorknob and turned it. My eyes widened as my lips sucked in air at surprise that the door would even be unlocked. Allowing the door to open a smidge, I peeked from behind my room's shadows, checking to see if the coast were clear. I could only see what the torches aligning the walls allowed, but from what I sensed it would be safe to exit.

Slipping from the room I closed the door behind me. With my body hunched over, I crept on my tiptoes down the hallway. The hallways were decorated like the previous one I had seen, with the red carpet running down the center. This hall smelled different though; while the previous hallway had no particular odor, this one smelled of incense.

I followed the fragrance of the incense down the hallway; it began to smell stronger the closer I came to a particular door. Keeping my body near the wall, I came to the room, incense rolled up from the bottom of the door. Calling myself a moron under my breath, I turned the knob of the door and allowed it to open just the tiniest bit.

Having placed my body in front of the cracked-open entrance, I began to breathe more heavily. The room I was looking into was not necessarily large, but it was long. I stood idle and scanned the room for occupancy for a few moments before letting the door drift open farther.

On my toes, I snuck farther into the dark chamber, closing the door behind me with my foot. The room was carpeted in dark maroon; shadows blocked me from viewing the walls, but at the end of the chamber was a Victorian bathtub. Candles circled the outside and rim of the bathtub, but nobody seemed to be in it. I inched myself closer until I was inches from the lit candles.

The water was dark, and vulture feathers blanketed the water's surface. I leaned over the bathtub, my fingers wrapping over the tub's rim. The tub felt warm to the touch, and I could feel tiny vapors rise from the still water that smelled of incense. Just when I had finally relaxed, an emergence of bubbles brought me back to reality. I focused my eyes and loomed my face closer to the water. Even though the water was colored dark, I could see the outline of a figure. The sight of an open-eyed old man startled me into jumping backwards and knocking over a candle in the process.

I just stared at the tub as the figure slowly rose from the water, feathers sticking to his skin. The old man was bald but had a thick and long white beard. The beard appeared like a wet cat hanging from his face, and his eyes were white with a thin black outline.

With regrets of entering the chamber, I stepped backwards. The old bearded man opened his mouth, and dark water poured from his lips. It was then that I realized the water was none other than his own blood.

"Don't go yet, Caleb."

I stopped in my tracks. I had reached the back of the chamber and fumbled at the wall with my hand behind me, looking for the handle. My hands froze as the old man announced the name that I myself had just learned was my own.

"Excuse me? Do you know me? Who told you my name?"

The old man smiled as a new wave of substance rushed from the corners of his mouth. He scratched at his bald head before allowing his arms to hang over the rim of the tub. I had found the doorknob and held it firmly in my hand, just in case this conversation became sour.

"These walls are thin, Caleb, and there is no such thing as a secret," the old man managed to spit out.

"So you make a habit out of eavesdropping. That's fine, perhaps you could help me out then?"

"Do you realize that you are naked?"

The old man had totally ignored my question and just commented on my nakedness. I had grown so used to not wearing clothes, but I suddenly realized my nakedness after his comment and jumped into the shadows and covered myself. The man laughed and clapped his hands together.

"I apologize; I did not mean to embarrass you," the old man said.

I tried to reply but only managed to release a few utterances.

"There are clothes on the chair behind you, if you're feeling chilly."

"What chair?" I replied.

A chair had appeared from thin air behind me. My back had been pressed against the wall a moment ago, but suddenly a chair leaned against my calves. I spun around quickly, and saw the dim outline of a wardrobe thrown over the back of the chair. The garments had a strange odor of smoked ham to them. I turned my head to eyeball the old man one more time; he had submerged almost his entire body into the tub, and only his eyes peeked at me from the water.

I turned back to the clothes, and even though I could not see them in the dark, I quickly put them on.

"Are you decent now, Caleb?"

"Yes," I replied while I pulled the top over my head.

"Good boy, now step on out here in the light. Let me take a look at you."

Nervous, I stepped into the candlelight. I looked down at my clothes and goosebumps covered my arms. I had on an old pair of gray Ohio State sweatpants and an old tank top. My head rose to look at the old man, and with a crooked smile the old bearded man chuckled.

"Who are you?" I muttered to the old man.

"I am nobody of importance at this time. There is much more to learn about the supernatural world than you think. There's more than one side to the dice."

It took a second to sink in, but the last line of the old man's sentence, caught my attention—that there was more than one side to the dice—those were the words Gadrel had spoken to me in the desert. I was prepared to ask the old man where he had heard that particular phrase when he dunked himself into the dark water, which caused wet feathers to flood over the rim, dousing a few candles out as well.

I ran over to the tub, tripping over the spilled liquid. With the combination of rushed movement and the slippery floor, my arms flew into the water. My eyes were wide and bloodshot, my mouth pulled back as if I had been riding a roller-coaster, and it took me a moment to catch some traction on the floor.

To my amazement the tub was empty. I rummaged at the bottom of the bathtub but felt nothing but feathers, and now the water had gone from warm to ice cold.

"What the hell was that?"

I stood up with my arms stained to the elbows in a dark red, and without thinking I wiped my face, trailing the red substance across my mug.

After processing what had just occurred I was prepared to leave the chamber when, with a large bang, the castle shook viciously. The tremor caused me to slip on the spilled water and crashed into the bathtub, and I busted my head open on the rim.

I jumped to my feet and slipped once more, so I crawled to the door on all fours. My clothes were soaked and darkened by the water, and I could hear loud noises and battle cries muffled from the distance. After I reached the door I swung it open, also still on my knees. Different figures sprinted down the hallways in both directions; their speed meant their identities were mere blurs to me.

Another explosion hit the castle, and a few of the running figures tripped and fell to their faces. Their faces were full of excitement and hunger, and although human in appearance their grins were full of three-inch fangs. Their eyes were round and large, and they all wore short tunics, which would be easy to fight in. With bald heads, they resembled piranhas.

Crawling into the hallway, I stood to my feet and quickly ran down the corridor. The doors that lined the hallway were all swung open, so as I made my way toward the back staircase I could peek into the rooms.

Most chambers were replicates of the fresco room Lacious left me in, but a particular room was full of the piranha men. At first I ignored the room and passed it up but then thought to myself and backpedaled to the doorway. There must have been five piranha men standing over tables full of weaponry.

I figured if I were to make it out of the castle, with whatever was happening outside, I would most likely benefit from being armed. Another explosion rattled the castle, and the piranha men cussed to themselves as they ran out of the room, armed to their teeth in blades and other blunt objects. After counting five men, I snuck into the room and ran to the table.

From left to right, any instrument of pain I could fathom rested on the table. Anything from simple blades to battle axes to a large mace were all available. I thought quickly and tucked a few daggers in my sweatpants' waistband. As I was about to leave, a shiny silver sword caught my attention from under the table. I could see the reflection of my grin in the sword's broad blade. Picking it up with one hand, it felt as light as a feather. After deciding to test it out, I raised it above my head and dropped it down upon the table. The table imploded down the middle, scattering weapons everywhere. With a nod of acknowledgment I grabbed the sword and ran from the room, braced for anything.

Dodging screaming piranha men, I reached the staircase and ran down them, skipping two steps at a time. Having reached the bottom, I found myself on the floor level. Exiting the staircase, I was in a large empty space which appeared to be a large court. Giant tapestries hung on the walls depicting demons and other idols. A black carpet ran from three thrones at the back of the court to the giant doors on the opposite end. Stunned, to say the least, I approached the center of the court when another explosion hit the castle.

I could now tell the giant doors of the court were at the receiving end of the impacts. The doors vibrated with violent force as another explosion hit them. Whatever was on the other side of those doors had to be a terrifying sight, with the intense sound of steel hitting steel, the cries of slaughtered men, and banshee-like screams, I assumed these were products of those nasty-looking piranha fighters.

Curious, I approached the door slowly, keeping my sword tight in hand. The castle rattled with another explosion, this time the door splintered down the center.

The next hit would most likely take the door out, so I got prepared to fight. The sound of feet averted my attention to behind me though; as I spun around, about a hundred of those piranha men stood in much better fighting stances than I could ever muster.

A bit relieved to see them, I figured I would no longer have to fight an oncoming ambush of men. That was until the piranha men created a half moon around me, spit flinging from their ugly teeth. I whispered to myself under my breath, "They think I'm the enemy."

The half moon began to close into a full circle, but as a final attack impacted the door, the piranha men found themselves ambushed by a mad rush of two hundred men. Splintered wood flew across the room as the flood of attackers merged with the piranhas into a chaotic mosaic of war. I used the deflection the piranhas offered as a chance to hide myself behind the court's thrones. I peered out from between two of the thrones and watched as the piranhas sunk their teeth into the flesh of the attackers, ripping off whatever they could bite into.

Men cut into the piranhas with extreme prejudice, smiling while they chopped their way through the packed court, not caring if they accidentally sliced into their own men.

The court was filled wall to wall with fighters. I watched twenty men drag a single piranha fighter to the center of the court, then take turns dicing into him with their hatchets.

I watched in horror the scene in front of me. I had no idea how long I would be safe hidden as I was, so I decided it perhaps I should return to the upper part of the castle.

A ten-foot gap separated me from the staircase, and I crawled to the end of the thrones and flexed my calves to get ready to run. I buckled my knee, lowered my level, and took a deep breath, but before I could even take off I felt a firm hand on my tank top.

I turned my head around to see bloodstained hands clutching the back of my tank top. Cane stared down at me with a smile on his face. "It would seem that we are always running into each other."

Not wanting to give him a chance for the first move, I erupted from my position and tackled Cane to the ground. Cane grabbed me by my ears and applied pressure to my lobes. Filled with fury, I shoved my thumbs into Cane's eye sockets. Cane screamed as I felt his eyes soften under my thumbs and I pushed in.

Releasing Cane I ran towards the staircase. After I jumped over a few fallen piranhas and Cane's men, I stopped at the stairway's entrance and turned back to see if I was being followed. Cane stood to his feet, his hands firmly against his face, and blood gushed from between his fingers.

Before I could even turn to get up the stairs, I came under attack by two piranhas. I swung at them, not realizing I lost my sword when fighting Cane; as a result I hit the first piranha with a weak uppercut. I thought fast and grabbed two daggers from my waistband, then cut the piranhas' throats. The two minions fell to their knees, clutching their blood-gushing throats.

Quickly I realized there would be no escape, and I was part of this fight. I found myself in the center of the court, cutting and stabbing whatever and whoever came near me. I was releasing noises and sounds I did not know were humanly possible.

No matter how many attackers I dropped dead or killed, the thicket of fighters were not thinning. They were not thinning, that is, until Lacious showed up.

The impressive tapestries had been ripped from the walls from the battle, covering a large proportion of fighters and influencing them to fight blindly. Bloodied bodies still crawled around the floor biting into ankles and hamstrings.

The piranhas' morale, which was falling, suddenly was renewed as Lacious flew through the broken doorway on his soul sucker. Cane's men looked in fear at Lacious, who calmly drifted above their heads.

With Lacious suddenly arriving I was in increased danger. I pushed myself to the back of the court as Lacious landed his soul sucker in the center of the court. The piranhas' chests heaved, while Lacious stepped down from his winged creature. The castle's attackers, as well as the piranhas, created a circle around Lacious, giving him plenty of room.

"I was wondering when you were going to make a move," Lacious shouted to the fighters.

"Now where is your leader Cane?"

I looked for Cane myself; I had lost track of him after our small tussle. My jaw dropped and I was in just as much astonishment as Lacious seemed to be at the sight of Cane slouched in the center throne. Blood ran down his face and spilled onto the clean marble throne.

"I am right here, Lacious."

I looked around to see the fighters' reaction to Cane. For the first time many of them realized Cane had been injured. Lacious stared at Cane in dismay.

"I did not think anyone would ever have the balls to sit in Lucifer's throne. That is something I didn't even think you'd dare to try, Cane," Lacious whispered loudly.

Cane bent over and grabbed his head in pain. His displaced eyes looked in awkward angles as he laughed.

"Shut up, Lacious. I've managed to penetrate your defenses, I've battled your royal guard and kept the upper hand, and now I sit in Lucifer's own throne. Where is your Master now, Lacious? I'll tell you where—he's afraid! He knows the support I have."

"You stupid fool. You had a good thing going for you; Lucifer was gracious enough to give you your own town. He pitied for you and your tribe, but what do you do? You decide to try and overthrow your Lord? What makes you think you'll even come close to a victory?" Lacious snarled.

Cane leaned back into the throne and gave a deep sigh. Rubbing his hands together, Cane put his arms behind his neck in an expression of relaxation.

"For one thing, Lacious, soon after I take care of you and your daddy Lucifer, I'll be taking Caleb for a little ride."

Lacious crossed his arms, ready to reply, when he paused. He suddenly dropped his arms to his side and his brow contorted in confusion.

"How are you familiar with Caleb? He was not aware of his identity until after Gadrel fetched him."

Cane grinned ear to ear, as he made a hissing sound.

"No, that is impossible. Tell me, Cane, where'd you learn of that?"

Lacious looked worried and anxious. The large court became filled with whispers between fighters and piranhas. Cane raised his arms to the air, and from the left Judas walked up and sat to Cane's right. Judas wore a gold tunic and no longer shuffled but had a strut to his walk, and as he sat down he grinned at Lacious with an expression of superiority.

Lacious growled under his breath and latched onto his dagger, ready to charge the two leaders of the rebellion. Lacious stopped in his tracks as he heard a hissing sound. Lacious looked behind him as he saw a yellow serpent slither out from the crowd of fighters. Everyone's eyes were on the serpent as it passed under Lacious's legs and onto the throne platform. Cane stood to his feet and chuckled to himself as he moved to the left throne, leaving the center throne empty.

The court held its breath as the serpent coiled itself onto the center throne.

"Please tell me this is another one of your jokes, Gadrel," Lacious muttered.

I could not believe my eyes. As I thought about it though, it began to make sense. Cane had spoken about having connections I would not believe. That is how it was so easy for Judas to break me out and how they were able to break into the castle so easily. Cane had recruited the help of Gadrel, apparently a powerful demon, or at least I assumed since he had the ability to strike such fear into Lacious.

The serpent rested on the center throne and smiled at Lacious, which caused Lacious's face to tighten in anger. Just as had happened in the desert, smoke began to rise from the serpent's scales. Judas kept his eyes on Lacious while Cane stared blindly into space. Like popcorn the scales popped from the serpent's body with a snapping sound; then, similar to those black snakes children ignite on the Fourth of July, white ash expanded from the serpent's body. The ash formed into the shape of a man; the figure fleshed out, which caused the entire court to watch in shock and awe.

I found myself short of breath as the serpent shaped into the old man I had seen in the bathtub earlier on. The old man's eyes shifted to me and gave me a quick wink before returning his sight to Lacious.

Lacious tossed his hair back, the green strands hitting his back with a heavy slap.

"Damn you, Gadrel, you have been up to something. Lucifer is going to have your hide for this one!"

Gadrel gripped his knees and leaned over. His white beard gently swayed in the light breeze that came from the court's broken down door. Gadrel slowly stuck out a long red tongue, which split into three forks. A low-pitched hiss expelled from his gaping grin.

As the hiss grew, the soul sucker resting behind Lacious began to get anxious. Its eyes rolled into the back of its head, while it began to dance in fear. Lacious spun around, startled as the soul sucker rose onto its hind legs and began to fling its lethal tail, which dissected half the crowd of fighters.

Lacious was wide-mouthed in astonishment as the soul sucker bulldozed him over and leaped into the air, escaping into the open sky. Gadrel leaned back in his seat and covered his mouth in chuckles.

"Are you seeing this, Cane?"

Cane turned his head to the voice of Gadrel. His bleeding sockets gave a stern expression to his appearance.

"That is so not funny, Gadrel. However, I am enjoying the sound of it. What do you say to finishing it?"

Gadrel patted Cane's hand, which gripped empty air. Cane rose to his feet and raised his arms to the sky, then dropped them down quickly, a movement I only could associate with a signal for attack.

Before Cane's hands even reached his side, his entire tribe of fighters that could still stand attacked Lacious in a massive push. Lacious roared, doing his best to rip into the body of men jumping at him.

I braced my body against the back of the court, which was now splattered entirely with sprinkles of blood and guts. Small puddles of blood were also scattered around the room; overzealous fighters easily slipped on the puddles and busted their heads on the hard pavement ground.

Eventually the dog pile of men thinned out, revealing Lacious riddled with stab wounds and laid out on the ground. He rose to his elbows and spit blood out onto himself. The thick red film covered his chin and lips in a gross manner as he swore at Gadrel in a language unknown to me.

Gadrel stood to his feet, and his flesh was wrinkled and covered in purple veins. He would have been naked if he was not wearing a white garment that resembled a dress. Gadrel strutted toward Lacious' beaten body, stepping into the remains of piranhas and Cane's men.

As he reached Lacious and sniffed the air around his body, he reached down and snatched the blade fallen by Lacious' side. Blood seeped from his stabbed body, as Gadrel leaned down on one knee and clutched Lacious by his hair.

Lacious' eyes appeared tired and heavy, and his pale face was almost transparent now. Gadrel placed the tip of the blade to Lacious' jugular.

"You've never been very fond of me, have you, Lacious?"

"What ever gave you that impression, Gadrel?" Lacious spit at Gadrel, splattering dots of blood against his wrinkled flesh.

Gadrel laughed while looking back at Judas and Cane. Judas was almost jumping in his seat with excitement, while Cane clenched his teeth in anger, furious he was not seeing the end of Lacious.

"That's very cute, Lacious. However, spitting on me is not what you should be doing right now."

"What would you suggest I do?"

"You should be begging to join my side. Where is your powerful Lucifer now? I knew I'd succeed but had no idea it would be this easy."

"Almost too easy, don't you think?" Lacious smiled.

Gadrel gave Lacious a curious look. "Where is Lucifer?"

Lacious closed his eyes, then opened them to Gadrel's astonishment. Lacious's eyes had turned red, and the bloodied open wounds that covered his body slowly began to close. Gadrel still had his green mess of hair locked in his fist but made a look of disgust as the back of Lacious's head softened up and his scalp peeled from his skull. Gadrel jumped to his feet and backpedaled toward the thrones. Judas gasped in horror, and with a rush of whispers and low screams Cane had reason to look alarmed as well.

"What is going on? Gadrel speak to me—what is happening?"

Cane looked around the court with his blind eyes. Judas tripped over his feet as he leaped up and ran into the stunned crowd of fighters.

"Judas, are you there? Somebody answer me, damnit!" Cane said with fear on his tongue.

Gadrel's wrinkled eyes thinned out, as Lacious crawled to his feet. The back of his head was in a pile on the ground. Lacious grabbed his face with his claw-like hand and peeled it away, revealing a black scaly skin.

I rubbed my eyes, attempting to figure out if I was seeing things or not, but to my dismay I was seeing no illusion. Gadrel lifted his hand to his mouth in surprise.

"No, it can't be. I would have known about this; this makes no logic!" Gadrel's voice rattled.

The Tribe of Cane began to step back slowly, while the court full of piranhas threw themselves to their knees. Gadrel's body trembled as he fell to the bloodied floor, throwing his arms down in submission. Gadrel lifted his eyes and saw the face of Lacious stuck to the ground in front of him. He raised his eyes to the figure in front of him, staring directly into Lucifer's eyes, begging for sympathy.

21. Trinity of Evil

Soon after Lacious peeled his face away to reveal himself as Lucifer, there was not much of a fight. Judas had escaped in the confusion, and as for Cane and his tribe, they surrendered. I do not know about Cane, but his men were sent to the abyss.

Lucifer found me cowered in the corner of the court and had a piranha escort me back to the chamber I had escaped. Much of what happened turned into one huge blur, so as I sat in the dark corner of my chamber, I just concentrated on what I should do next.

I was not alone for too long when I heard the doorknob turn and the sound of the door swinging open. I lifted my head to see Aziel standing in the doorway; the hallway backlit him, so shadows hid his face.

"I heard I missed quite the party."

"Yes you did, and you're not one to miss a party, Stranger."

Aziel stepped into the room, and the door closed behind him automatically. He leaned against the back wall and crossed his arms. His lips puckered and forehead relaxed, Aziel sighed.

"My name is Aziel."

I rolled my eyes, not fully accepting that all the angelic qualities of Stranger had been lost.

"What is going to happen to Gadrel? I mean, I'm usually always confused, but he even looked shaken up after Lacious ripped his own face off."

Aziel tapped his foot on the floor. I sat cross-legged and looked toward the black marble ground, chuckling softly to myself.

"What do you find humorous?"

"Oh, it's really nothing. It's just whenever something crazy happens, a pattern has grown to where I end up sitting with you, and you end up explaining things, then suddenly everything makes sense."

Aziel smirked and walked closer to me. His cape still lightly flew in an invisible wind as he knelt down to eye level with me.

"You may know a man named St. Thomas Aquinas. He was a fan of Aristotle's theories and believed the man upstairs created both reason and divine knowledge. He believed they went hand in hand and therefore could not contradict one another. However, he also stated what cannot be explained by reason can still be true and must be accepted by faith."

"You lost me at Aristotle."

Aziel laughed; the smile on his face was a faint hint of what used to be his angelic quality, but if he could still smile, perhaps there still existed a chance to save him.

"Thomas Aquinas said that there exist things such as the trinity, or other religious doctrines, that surpass human reason and understanding. Therefore since they expand beyond human logic, it is impossible for a human to grasp them."

"Thomas Aquinas is a deep thinker, but that still doesn't help me understand the Lucifer and Lacious connection."

"That's the point," Aziel laughed.

I grunted to myself and rested my head against the wall behind me. Aziel sighed and sat on his butt in front of me, wrapping his arms around his knees.

"Do you remember the concept of the Trinity? Also, the conversation we had once involving it?"

My interest was piqued. I sat up straight and thought back to conversations we had had. I suddenly did remember a conversation in which I wondered if Lucifer could have a trinity of his own, some sort of trinity of evil.

"Yes, I do remember a conversation like that," I said.

"Then wrap your mind around this. Lucifer and Lacious are the same person."

My head started to hurt again. "So Lacious is the son of Lucifer?"

"No, not exactly."

"That makes no sense at all; I have seen them both in the same room multiple times. There's no way they can be the same person."

"That is exactly the point. You cannot understand it because it is beyond your logic. That is another thing that bothers many spiritual beings about humans, that they try to grasp spiritual knowledge through human reason. Doing that is like trying to put out a fire with gasoline."

"Well, all I know is Gadrel looked pretty damn surprised."

"Gadrel is special."

"What do you mean by special?"

Aziel got to his feet and dusted off his hands. He started walking toward the door, hesitating for a second to turn and speak. "That story is far too long to tell."

Aziel left the chamber, shutting the door behind him. I was once again alone with only the shadows to keep me company. My eyes roamed the room endlessly, until the door opened once more. I figured it would be Stranger again, but to my surprise, Cane was thrown into my chamber.

He cried out, while his hands waved in front of him. The chamber door slammed behind him as he walked into a wall. He looked terrible; his tunic was in shreds, and a piece of it was wrapped around his eyes.

"Hello, is anybody there?"

I slowly stood to my feet and knocked on the plaster wall. Cane jumped, and his body tensed up.

"Who is that? C'mon, speak up."

I crept up on Cane, as he was now spinning in circles with his arms waving out, attempting to feel for anything. I lowered my position and jabbed him in the gut with my forefinger. Cane screamed and jumped backwards, swinging his arms like a madman.

"Who are you? What are you doing?"

I played with him for a bit longer, jabbing him with my fingers and watching him scream and jump around. Eventually I grew tired of the game and kicked him in the back of his legs, buckling him to the floor.

Cane's kneecaps smashed into the marble floor with a loud crack of breaking bones. I covered my mouth in shock, since I had not meant to do that much damage to him. Cane fell on his face, shouting in pain. I ran back to my corner, expecting Stranger or a piranha to come see what the loud noise was. When nobody came and Cane stopped crying, I approached him again.

"Hello Cane."

Cane looked up, although I did not know why he even bothered. He reached out toward me, not having the ability to stand.

"Caleb, is that you?" Cane whined.

"Yes, it is me. Why are you talking to me in a tone you'd use with a friend?"

"Oh man, don't tell me you're still bitter about the betraying-you thing. Can't you forgive me?"

I rolled my eyes and sat against the wall. I found watching Cane in such terrible shape somewhat fulfilling, and that disturbed me.

"What happened to Napoleone?" I asked.

"Well, we cut off his head."

"You did what?" I said in shock.

Cane resembled a worm, squirming on the floor blindly.

"Give me a break, Caleb; it's not as if I killed him, at least not in the sense of human murder."

"Please Cane, I can't deal with any more beyond human understanding conversations."

"What are you talking about?" Cane now rested his cheek against the cold floor.

"Never mind; why are you not in the abyss?" I asked Cane.

Cane rolled himself onto his back, his legs mangled under him. I traced the white swirls in the marble with my index finger as Cane mumbled silently, "I don't even care anymore."

Before I could reply the door opened and Stranger, or should I say Aziel, stepped in. He took a glance at the mangled Cane and smirked. "We're leaving, and now you get to carry him."

I leaped up and shot Aziel a dirty look. "I'm not carrying him, and where exactly are we going?"

Fumes expelled from the corners of Aziel's mouth. He narrowed his brow and growled under his breath. "You will carry him, and don't worry about where we're going."

Not wanting to be burned to a crisp, I spit out a few choice words under my breath and walked over to Cane. I lifted him onto my shoulders; his weight bogged me down to a painful slouch, and his legs would bounce and hit my calves at every pace, which became very annoying.

"Last time you said that, I ended up with Jack the Ripper," I muttered under my breath.

I followed Aziel down the hall and down the staircase. After two flights the weight of Cane was unbearable, I could not go on anymore.

"Stranger, I mean Aziel, I can't carry him anymore. Not down all these flights."

Aziel turned around and looked up at me. He rubbed his chin, then when he reached a decision he pointed down the balcony.

"Drop him then, we'll collect him at the bottom."

Cane's head perked up faster than a groundhog's.

"What did you say?"

Without a word, I agreed with Aziel and dumped Cane over the railing. His body went flying down the ten flights before smashing at the land level. My chest heaved, as I was finally able to catch my breath. Aziel shook his head and chuckled. "I was kidding by the way."

I was too out of breath to reply, so I just followed Aziel down the remaining flights. When we reached the bottom, Cane moaned from beneath his busted teeth. Aziel picked him up, and threw him over his left shoulder; Cane's teeth fell from his gums and scattered along the ground.

We stood in the court. The place was spotless now, not an ounce of blood could be seen on the floor or walls, although the court's titanic-sized door still remained busted down the center and left split open. Battle-bruised piranhas hung on the walls, hanging back up the giant tapestries.

Aziel and I strolled across the court and through the mammoth doors. As I stepped outside, the orange sky was burning with heat. Instantly sweat began to perspire from my forehead and palms.

We walked for a while in awkward silence. I felt a need to fill the air with at least some form of conversation, and there was one thing I was curious about.

"Aziel, about this Unholy Trinity again, in the Holy Trinity there's the Holy Ghost, so what, is there an unholy ghost or something?"

Cane's head bounced against Aziel's cape, while Aziel shot me a look of intrigue.

"I guess you could call it a lesser form of possession. You always hear about worshipers being overcome with the Holy Spirit. It's a similar idea; for instance, one can be overcome with what would be better called the Sadistic Sense."

Nodding my head, we continued to walk at least a mile. My clothes were heavy in sweat, and dirt clung to my perspiring feet in large clumps. Eventually we reached the destination to which Aziel was apparently taking us.

I became somewhat nervous at the sight of fifty piranhas circled ten yards in front of us. Their backs were turned, and they seemed to be holding something down. As we approached closer, a few of the piranhas spread open and revealed Gadrel being held captive by huge chains.

Gadrel was no longer in the shape of an old man but returned to the winged being with horns I had run into in the desert. My spine began to itch as I became more nervous. Gadrel growled, vapors expelling from his mouth that smelled of burning coal.

I paid so much attention to Gadrel I had not realized there was a circular hole in the ground, maybe fifteen feet in circumference, with a metal plate on top of it.

The piranhas continued to wrestle with the chained Gadrel; his chain was glowing red with the heat conveying off his body. Aziel let out a breath, and tossed Cane to the ground. He strolled over to the metal plate and lifted it up and off the hole, placing it to the side for a moment. Cane moved his head side to side, most likely disoriented.

"What are you doing, Caleb?"

Trading glances between Gadrel struggling with fifty piranhas and Aziel, who now loomed over Cane, I was torn with curiosity.

"Cane, I've got some bad news for you. As a result of attempting to overthrow the power and authority of Lucifer, you are being cast away to the abyss. That's right, you are being banished yet again from the opposite side of spiritual power," Aziel laughed.

Cane's mouth trembled; blind and discontent, he could not muster up the words he wanted to say. Aziel lifted Cane to the air and walked him to the edge of the dark abyss. Lifting him into the air, Aziel spoke some words that sounded Latin before dropping Cane. Cane's head hit the rim of the hole, which busted his head open before he went plummeting down into the dark and cold abyss. I could hear Cane scream until his voice faded into nothing. Aziel shrugged his shoulders and spun around to face me. I stepped back, afraid I was next.

"No Aziel, don't throw me back down there," I pleaded.

"Calm down, Caleb, I'm not tossing you into the abyss. We're not finished with you yet. I brought you only to watch."

Although Aziel reassured me he was not tossing me into the abyss, I still took the time to separate the two of us farther. Aziel now directed his attention toward Gadrel.

"Bring him forward," Aziel commanded to the piranhas.

The fifty piranhas moved as a unit and inched Gadrel closer to the rim of the abyss. Gadrel fought with all his might, attempting to wrestle out of his chains. Aziel casually walked over to Gadrel and grabbed him by the cheeks. He leaned in and whispered—he must have not wanted me to hear what he was saying, but I cupped my ears and managed to barely make it out anyway.

"What did you do with the tree? We'll pardon you, if you just tell us where the tree is," Aziel whispered softly.

Gadrel stared eye to eye with Aziel, his eyes changing hues of blue.

"I will never tell you, Aziel," Gadrel snarled, some spit flying from his mouth onto Aziel's face.

Aziel wiped off his face and stepped back, flinging his cape over his shoulders.

"Fine, no more wasting time then. Throw him down there." Aziel pointed toward the abyss.

The piranhas wrestled to inch Gadrel closer but could not overcome his strength. Gadrel whipped his body like a lunatic, and a few of the piranhas tripped and fell down the hole themselves. Aziel raised his eyebrows as the piranhas huddled in on Gadrel and with all their united might attempted to shove him down the abyss.

"How long are you going to fight, Gadrel?"

Gadrel stopped fighting. He stood still as a marble statue and just stared at Aziel. His bottom lip trembled with anger and frustration.

"Send Lucifer a message for me, Aziel. Tell him he has not seen the last of Gadrel."

After that remark, Gadrel leaped himself into the abyss. He had leaped with such speed and might that he dragged all fifty piranhas with him down into the darkness. Aziel dusted off his shoulders and placed the metal plate back over the abyss, covering it for the time being.

22. Dinner with the Devil

I was seated in a large dining room decorated with mahogany wood. At the left of the room, which was half the size of a football field, was a large gothic-style window. Through the window the burning orange sky leaked into the room, which caused the stone floor to appear to glow.

The dining room was cold, and a light haze circulated the air. I was seated at a table, maybe thirty yards long. The oversized chair made me feel like a child since my legs dangled over the seat, hovering over the ground by about eight inches.

For the moment I was alone. I had been seated in the dining room alone ever since Aziel brought me back to the castle. Bored out of my mind and utterly frustrated, I decided to explore the room a bit by myself. I jumped off the chair and walked slowly around the room, my bare feet made a slap-like stepping noise that echoed against the cathedral ceiling.

"Hello, Caleb." I heard a voice from across the room speak to me.

After I spun around, I curled my toes and nodded my head toward Lucifer, who had addressed me from the head of the dining table.

"I didn't even see you come in," I replied to Lucifer.

Lucifer wore a suit with black pinstripes down the jacket, which looked as if it were about to bust open at any moment around his massive body. His beady red eyes looked through me, while he motioned for me to sit at the chair next to him.

"Will you join me for dinner, Caleb?"

Lucifer sat himself down at the head of the table. He opened the napkin that was placed on his saucer and covered his lap with it. Nervous and suspicious, I crept to the table and crawled onto the oversized chair.

Figuring I would humor him, I covered my lap with my napkin as well. Looking at Lucifer's legs, he also appeared child-like in the massive chairs we were seated in. He had noticed my eyes on him and swung his legs like an infant would and chuckled.

"You know, Caleb, we could be friends."

"Excuse my reluctance, Lucifer, if I just don't trust you."

Lucifer sat up straight and took a deep breath that caused a button to pop from his shirt.

"That is sad to hear, Caleb, it really is. Would you like something to eat?" Lucifer asked me.

"To tell you the truth, I've been starving so long it almost feels natural now."

"That's never good to hear; let us remedy that. What do you say?" Lucifer snapped his fingers, and a servant scurried into the room.

I looked at the servant; it was a woman with a wrinkled appearance and bags under her eyes. She stood with her back straight and her arms wrapped behind her.

"What can I get you, sir?" the servant addressed me.

I kind of liked the feeling of being called sir. Lucifer gave me a quick wink and then ordered us some food.

"Go fetch us some nice juicy steaks. How does that sound, Caleb?"

I must have looked lost; I bounced my foolish expression toward the servant and nodded my head, saliva dripping from the corners of my mouth. "That would be divine."

I could see Lucifer flinch at the dictation I used, but I pretended not to notice it. The servant bowed her head and scurried from the room.

"Now back to business, Caleb. I'm not as bad of a guy as people make me out to be. I mean, I'm really not; I am blamed for a lot of things that I have no hand in at all. The big man upstairs runs into a similar problem as well. Whenever somebody dies young, or even just dies, what is the first thing people say?"

"They ask, 'Why God?'" I answered.

Lucifer snapped his fingers and pointed at me with a sly smirk.

"Exactly, that's what I'm talking about. Now, was it the big man upstairs who murdered their child or allowed their children to become kidnapped?" Lucifer asked me.

"No, I wouldn't say that."

"Of course you wouldn't. If it was true, and a young child being murdered and raped was part of a divine plan, what would make the difference between good from evil? Not to mention as well, if God did evil things, such as have some family's only place to live burnt down, in order to fulfill a larger scheme of things, that would contradict the idea of free will. Did those people choose to have their house burnt down so His plan could be reached?"

I sat quietly in my seat and let Lucifer continue to give me his speech. His hands moved wildly in the air as he spoke to me, and his beady eyes lit up with enthusiasm.

"So just as God cannot be blamed for humans' misfortunes, I cannot either."

"There is a difference though between the two of you. You're the devil, that's your job."

Lucifer held onto his stomach as he bent over in a painful outburst of laughter. When he finally settled down, the servant had arrived with our food. As she placed the mouth-watering steak in front of me, the smell attacked my nostrils violently. Saliva poured from my mouth, as I grabbed onto the steak and ripped my teeth, which had been suffering from malnutrition, into the steak. The meat tasted so bloody and juicy I just sucked onto it like it was a sponge before chewing it. Lucifer rubbed his chin as he watched me rip into my steak like a fiendish animal. Grabbing onto a fork and knife Lucifer began to eat his steak as well. We sat in silence, well except for my growls of pleasure in between bites, and ate our dinners. After I finished most of my meal, Lucifer looked at me and his thin brows furrowed.

"I'm curious, Caleb, why would the misfortunes of people be my job? Wouldn't that imply I'd be working for a power of good?"

With my mouth stuffed with steak, I was nearly out of breath from eating so fast, but I managed to get a few words out.

"Well it makes sense," I said, food falling from my mouth.

"Or perhaps that's the only reason you can think of," Lucifer replied, biting a chunk of steak off his fork.

I ate my steak like a cow, while I felt an awkward vibe from Lucifer. "What other reason would there be?" I asked.

Lucifer plucked a piece of meat from his teeth before answering me. "There might be the select few cases, in which I was directly responsible for a person's outcome, but for the most part, people's damnation is by their own hands.

"Listen to me ramble; I'm getting off subject. I invited you to dinner, Caleb, not to debate theology but to offer you once more a position at my side. I mean in reality your only choice is how easy you'll make my job get done. It might as well benefit you since you have no choice."

I swallowed the last piece of steak and wiped my bloodied mouth with the sleeve of my arm. I looked around the room for a few moments, attempting to avoid having to answer Lucifer's question.

"I see that you are still on the fence about it. Well allow me to let you be alone and think it over; in fact I'll send out some dessert for you. You should know where to find me, Caleb."

Lucifer jumped from the chair and adjusted his tie before walking toward the exit. He left, and I sat there alone until the servant came back with a covered dessert plate. She put it down in front of me and smiled.

"What is it?" I asked her.

The servant put her finger against her lip, signaling for me to be silent. Then with her other hand, she gripped the top and lifted it from the plate. I jumped back, knocking my chair to the ground and hitting my head against the stone floor.

What rested on the dessert plate, decorated with strawberries, was the Persian's head.

23. Possessed

I had run from the dining room back into the hallway, my legs flailing behind me, and threw myself against the brick wall; the steak I had eaten moments ago upheaved itself onto the wall. The meaty chunks I had swallowed whole trailed down the bricks and formed clumps on the floor.

I bent over and held onto my stomach, spitting out the few remaining pieces from my mouth, and groaned with my eyes closed. Lucifer had definitely gotten his point across. There I was, thinking he was just offering me a nice dinner, but he wanted to make it clear who is in charge.

The servant who had brought me the Persian's head approached me from behind. She looked at my vomit in disgust and patted me on my back, as I was still attempting to collect myself.

"Are you all right, sir? You rushed out without finishing."

I looked at the woman and wiped the slime from my lower lip. "I'll be fine; thank you though."

Suddenly the woman raised a brown paper bag to my face. It appeared to have a heavy object inside of it.

"What is that?" I asked.

"Well you left without eating; this is your doggy bag, sir," the servant replied.

Grabbing onto my mouth, I ran down the hallway not wanting to puke any more than I already had. I ran until I reached a part of the castle I had not been in before. I slowed my pace, cleaning my wet hand on my sweatpants, as I ventured through the new corridor.

I stared down the hallway, and my jaw dropped when Judas walked out of one of the rooms, crossed the hallway, and entered the opposite door. I heard the door close behind him and decided to see what was going on, shocked at the mere fact he was still in the castle after the incident he pulled. I remembered seeing him run away during the attack on Lucifer but never thought he would stay in the castle, let alone roam the place alone.

I crept up to the door and pressed my ear close to the wood. I could hear the faint sound of voices inside. The voices were distorted through the wood, so I could only come to the conclusion that there were two individuals in the room.

As the doorknob turned, I quickly launched myself backwards into the room across the hall, the one which Judas had exited earlier. I kept the door open just by a hairline and watched Aziel leave the room.

After the sound of Aziel's footsteps disappeared I crossed the hall and entered a tan room with old rugs thrown on the floor. The ceiling was painted black, and Judas was tied to a chair in the corner of the chamber. I gave him an analyzing stare, confused at his current actions.

"What are you thinking? Why would you stick around here, Judas? Are you really that stupid?" I asked him, talking with my hands.

Judas gave me a confused look. He furrowed his eyebrows, which brought them together looking like a burnt caterpillar. The chair he was tied up on was made of rough wood, his arms were behind his back, and his ankles were tied to the rear legs of the chair.

"Trust me, this is not the position I'd prefer to be in," Judas replied.

"You have some nerve showing your face here, Judas. A coward like you should be halfway to the other side of Hell by now."

I stepped behind Judas and kicked the back of his chair. He hollered as he went face first onto the nasty rugs that covered the ground. The chair tipped over, so Judas's knees pointed toward the wall.

"What are you doing? Are you insane?" Judas yelled.

"You betrayed me!" I screamed out.

"No I didn't," Judas replied with his teeth clenched.

Tired of his antics, with a roll of my eyes I left the room. I was about to storm off but suddenly began to feel curious as to the reason Aziel was speaking with Judas in the first place. Allowing the curiosity to get the better of me, I strolled back into the room and picked Judas's chair up.

"What were you and Aziel talking about?" I asked.

"How does that concern you? I don't even know who you are," Judas replied.

I was alarmed at Judas's comment. He had no reason to lie about such a thing as that. I leaned in, looking deep into Judas's eyes. He did look different, almost as if a different energy was inside him.

"You don't remember me?" I asked.

"I saw you once before. You were in a cage though, inside Lacious's chamber. I'll admit I felt sorry for you at first, but now I'm leaning the other way."

My mind began to race. I attempted to think back to when I first was stuck in that cage, being hounded by Lucifer and Lacious, who sent Judas to go fetch Aziel.

"My name is Caleb. So you don't remember anything?"

"Your name is Caleb? Now that you mention your name, Aziel had mentioned you."

"What did he say?"

"Not much, now can you get me out of these ropes? I'm not taking part in Aziel's sick plans anymore."

"I cannot believe this," I simply replied.

Judas opened his mouth, but before he could spill out a sentence I had left the room. At first I walked at a steady pace, but I quickened my strokes until I was at a full-out sprint.

I had come to know the castle well by now. Every exit was guarded by a small army of piranhas, which guaranteed me no escape. Lucifer kept himself to his own private wing, and Aziel had his own room at the west side of the northeastern tower.

By the time I had reached the tower in which Aziel rested, my chest was heaving and my hands shook anxiously. I climbed up a few flights and busted open Aziel's chamber door without hesitation. Aziel's chamber was small and plain. There were no decorations or furniture. The only item in the room was a single flower in a vase placed on the wall's mantle.

Aziel leaned against his wall, his nose to his flower when I burst into his chamber. He turned his head and smiled at me, his pointy grin welcoming me.

"Can I help you, Caleb?" Aziel asked.

I tried my best to speak, but being out of breath, I had to fight for every word. "What game are you playing, Aziel, and why did you not let me in on it?"

"I don't know what you're talking about, Caleb."

Aziel turned his head back away from me. His red skin stuck out like a sore thumb in such a light-colored room.

"Just admit it, Aziel; you're playing both sides of the fence."

"You have no idea what I am playing," Aziel growled.

"Yes I do, Aziel. You have been possessing Judas as a puppet to your own scheme!" I accused him.

"How can you prove it? Even if you could, who would you tattle me out to, Caleb?"

I closed the door behind me and leaned myself against it. Pressing my weight into the door, and lowering my voice as if I were telling a secret, I spoke to Aziel.

"I'll say I was wrong if you can answer one question."

"Okay, ask the question," Aziel replied.

"When the castle was attacked by the Tribe of Cane, where were you? You were nowhere to be seen. You would think when the castle of Lucifer is under attack, an entity such as yourself, who knows nothing but the art of protecting, would be there to fight."

Aziel moved his eyes onto me, licking his lips and rubbing his dry hands together, sending flakes of skin swirling in spirals to his feet. "So you think I was gone because I was controlling Judas at the time? Now what would I achieve by that?"

"That is an easy one Aziel; first off you would eliminate all threats that pose serious danger to you or whatever plan you might have up your sleeve. Second, you would get rid of Gadrel," I answered.

"Now you see there, why would I want Gadrel gone?" Aziel asked me.

"Why you would want Gadrel gone? I couldn't tell you to be positive. I bet though it has something to do with that tree I heard you whispering about."

By the expression on Aziel's face at the mention of Gadrel's tree, I knew I had struck a nerve. "I'm right, aren't I? This all has something to do with a tree. I can tell by the look on your face, Aziel."

I crossed my arms and puckered my face, knowing I was onto something big. Aziel sighed and relaxed his posture. He looked at me and stepped closer, which made me a bit nervous. Mocking my composure he narrowed his eyes and asked me, "What can you remember about your life, Caleb?"

Thinking hard, I shut my eyes in order to concentrate better. A few select fundamental memories surfaced up, including my name.

"My name is Caleb Stone and I worked as a reporter."

"Is that all you can remember, Caleb? Nothing else pops up into your memory?"

"Well, just the most basic things I find I am able to remember. Why are you asking me this and changing the subject?"

"This has everything to do with the subject at hand, Caleb."

Aziel stepped closer to me and pressed his palm against my forehead. Steam rose from between his fingers as my marking burned into his demon flesh. An extraordinary thing happened though; my thinking started to become clearer and clearer, and I began to remember details of my life instead of only mundane facts.

"All right, now tell me what you remember," Aziel directed.

With steam still rising from his palm, Aziel took his hand away from my head. I felt color coming back to my skin, as I could now narrate parts of my life.

"I can remember so much more of my life now, Aziel. I was a reporter for the local newspaper of my town; I mainly reported on town events, and every now and then I wrote an opinionated piece on a national issue.

"It's all coming back now. I went to work for another news company. It took me years to be offered a job by them, but once I was on their staff they sent me to the Middle East to cover the war."

Aziel once again leaned against the mantle. He nodded his head and crossed his legs as he stood. "Now tell me about the tree."

"Let me think, it's still a little vague. It was my first piece, and I wanted to make a name for myself. My contact in the country suggested I not get to close to the action, but the eagerness and overzealous nature I had as a reporter caused me to do stupid things.

"Most of the fighting I had learned was over a small piece of Holy Land. When I say small, I'm not exaggerating either. What the two sides were fighting over was a small Rowan tree which was considered to be the holiest of trees to the two factions.

"The fighting went on for weeks, and I was at ground zero throughout the entire duration. I can still smell the rotting flesh of the fighters. Bodies were left in the street as silent threats to the opposing forces.

"There was no water supply either; the people of the area were uneducated, and if it was wet, they considered it drinkable. This resulted in epidemics of diarrhea and illness, and flies were as common as birthmarks.

"I felt as if I were in Hell. Wow, that is a strange to say while standing in Hell right as I say it. After two months of hunger and drinking stagnant water, I no longer had the passion I had arrived with. It appeared as if the people were bent over slaughtering each other for a tree, a single tree."

I slid down the wall and sat on my floor, my legs stretched out. The memory of the situation, all the death I had seen, flooded back to me in painful waves. Aziel gave me a look of understanding.

"So you can see how a tree can be so important?" Aziel asked.

I was confused. "What do you mean? What about the tree?"

"You had to write an article, right? Why did they believe in being so dedicated to winning a simple tree?"

"Well, the local fighters believed it was the Tree of Knowledge. They thought it was the location of the Garden of Eden. I don't understand though; the tree was destroyed during the conflict. I went home a few weeks after it disappeared."

"How do you know it was destroyed, Caleb? Did you see it explode?"

"Well no," I replied.

"Then how do you know it was destroyed then?"

"It was assumed. Both sides denied they had possession of the Rowan tree, and neither would have dared move it from its location; it was considered too holy."

"So that makes sense? They wouldn't move it, but they'd destroy it?" Aziel laughed.

"It could have been by accident, Aziel."

Aziel bent down in order to look into my eyes better. His eyes penetrated me with a deep glare.

"There existed two trees in the Garden of Eden. The first was the Tree of Life, which was planted in order to give humans eternal life. The second tree was the Tree of Knowledge, planted by Gadrel himself. Gadrel was the serpent in the tree, which seduced Eve into biting the fruit of knowledge."

"That was stupid of her," I stuck my two cents in.

Aziel shot me a questioning gaze. "And you did not fall for his charm?"

Aziel's comment shut me up.

"The Tree of Life would guarantee the eternal life and peaceful existence of human beings as long as it stood. Sadly, resentment and revenge are innate to the nature of man, angry at God; the Tree of Life was chopped down, ending peace and immortality forever.

"The Tree of Knowledge, which damned man from creation, would stand for thousands of years—that is, until it disappeared, but not by the hand of man."

"Is that really bad? I mean, who cares if it disappeared?"

"It was enough to get the attention of the boss. The only one that might have the answers needed was Gadrel."

"Didn't you like just throw him into the abyss? How's that going to get answers for you?"

"You're correct in that having him answer a few questions would have been mighty useful. However, it's no longer necessary. You've got all that's needed for now."

"What's that, may I ask?"

"You bit into the Fruit of Knowledge; you have the seed of the tree in your stomach," Aziel said as he grinned and I scooted over so he could leave the room.

As he left the chamber, I sighed with relief from recovering some history of my life. I was beginning to form a sense of identity. Perhaps I had not been sold out, after all, but was chosen for a larger plan, for a greater good—maybe a confusing, drawn-out master scheme nobody let me in on, but a master plan nonetheless.

Suddenly I realized, though, the seed Aziel spoke of was most likely expelled from my body earlier, when I puked all over the dining room corridor.

24. Caleb's End

I cannot understand why good news can never arrive alone. Gadrel was right in saying that there were more sides to the dice I had been rolling than I had originally thought. Recently finding out that there had been a hidden purpose behind Aziel selling me out to Lucifer, I felt more positive about my odds of survival. On the other hand, my only contribution to Aziel's quest I had just puked up.

Having very little choice, I had left Aziel's chamber and quickly paced myself back to the dining hall. The castle's hallways had a damp feel to them, which caused the remaining hairs on my arm to stand up on end.

I reached the dining hall's corridor and tried to look for my pile of puke. From what I could remember, the puke would have to be someplace close to the dining room's doorway. I scanned the entire floor and walls but could not find a speck of my dinner anywhere.

Not finding anything, I entered the dining room and saw a couple of servants setting places at the long table. It did not take long for them to take notice of my presence, so that they stopped their activities and stood at attention.

"May we be of service to you, sir?" one said to me.

Random noises escaped from my lips before I could coherently gather my thoughts. There was no delicate way of saying what I needed to be said.

"Has anyone seen my puke?"

I expected the servants to roll their eyes or shoo me away with their hands. To my surprise though, one of the servants scurried away into what I would only assume to be the kitchen's doorway. She shortly reappeared with a doggy bag, then returned to setting forks in place around the table.

Approaching the brown paper bag, I could tell the bottom of the bag was wet and soft, probably ready to fall into pieces at the moment I picked up. I did not feel like carrying a bag of vomit around the castle's hallways, so right at the table I opened up the bag and stuck my hand inside.

One of the male servants, who had his head shaved and wore a shredded tunic, turned his attention to me. He stared at me with a furrowed expression and tightened his nose at the wet slurping noises my fingers made while slapping through the bag of stomach acid.

Having fingered through some large chucks of meat, I soon came to the understanding it would be impossible to tell a seed from anything else. I shot my eyes up toward the two servants watching me with their jaws dropped, as I lifted the bag to my mouth and swallowed my cold clumpy puke.

It tasted of spoiled matter, and hung for a few moments at the back of my throat. The vomit was cold, and parts were hard to swallow, which required additional chewing. Eventually though, I succeeded in finishing the entire bag.

I tossed the bag onto the table and rubbed my belly. A belch escaped my throat, which burnt my lower tongue and irritated my chapped lips.

"You must have been hungry, sir," the female servant said.

Wiping my mouth off with my hand, I smiled at the servants before I turned to exit the room. I had gotten two steps into the hallway, when I had to grab my throat in order to keep myself from puking my vomit up once again.

Feeling utterly disgusted, I decided to retire to my chamber. I took my time to walk back to my room, paying extra attention to the smack of my bare feet against the red carpet as I walked. Finally reaching my chamber, I was alarmed to find the door swung open halfway.

I outstretched my hand to swing the door open fully, and could see I had visitors. Twenty piranhas stood at attention against the far wall. One of the piranhas, who wore a red scarf around his wrist stepped forward. Drool leaked from between his jagged teeth, and a large infected scar swooshed across his face.

"Can I help you?" I asked the lead piranha.

"It's time for you to come with us," the piranha said as he gripped onto my shoulder.

The other nineteen piranhas chopped their jaws, most likely hoping I would not go in peace. However, I felt secure the odds were with me, so I allowed them to take me away without a fight. With two of the escorts on either side of me, the head piranha led the way, as the rest of the henchmen tagged behind.

We detoured through the library, which was a large room holding thousands of scrolls and documents, and ended up in the main court. The piranhas lined up, and I was thrown to my knees at the front of the line. My knees cracked at contact with the hard floor, and I clenched my teeth together, nearly biting my tongue in the process.

I looked up to see Lucifer relaxed on the center throne, a black cape around his neck. His massive build filled the throne and spilled over onto the thrones on either side of him. Standing behind Lucifer's throne was Aziel. Aziel looked at me with a stern face and winked his left eye.

"Hello Caleb, I hope the dessert I had prepared for you was to your expectations," Lucifer laughed.

I tried to stand, but the piranha who held firmly onto my shoulder shoved me back to my knees.

"So, what is your answer, Caleb? There is no more stalling. I need an answer now."

Clenching my fists, I spit at Lucifer and was able to make contact with his feet. Lucifer shook his head, as one of his henchmen ran up and licked the mess from his toes.

"I guess that's a no," Lucifer said to me.

"I will never help you get into Heaven."

"Yes you will, even if it's not you entirely. I think I've been amazingly patient with you, Caleb. Wouldn't you agree, Aziel?"

"Yes, you have," Aziel said, keeping his eyes concentrated on me.

"Thank you, Aziel. Now Caleb, I was hoping you'd learn to get along with me; I could have made you a very powerful man. Instead though you succeeded only in helping a flood of revolts rise. It's crazy to even think the poor fools who now lay at rest in the abyss thought they stood a chance up against me.

"The important thing to remember though, Caleb, is I have more than one way to break your stubbornness. Aziel, will you now take over from here?"

I did not know what Lucifer meant by what he said to Aziel, but I had to admit it did make me nervous. Aziel strolled around the three thrones and stepped in front of me.

"What is all this?" I asked to Aziel.

Lucifer chuckled to himself and felt obligated to fill me in, even though I directed my question toward Aziel.

"All we need is your soul, boy. Aziel here is going to take possession of your body so as to control you but still have your soul reside inside of you. Aziel, you have proven yourself very loyal to me; I will reward you greatly once those gates are open."

"Thank you, Lucifer," Aziel replied.

Aziel turned himself back to me and placed his hands on my shoulders. He looked into my eyes and sighed as he leaned in.

"Relax, and trust me," Aziel whispered in my ear.

"Is it going to hurt?" I asked quietly.

But suddenly before Aziel could take possession of my body, a piranha suddenly stormed into the court with Judas in his clutches. Lucifer jumped up to his feet and stared at Judas with a look that could kill.

"What is he doing here?" Lucifer roared.

"I found him tied up in one of the private chambers. He has some important information to tell you, he says," the piranha replied.

"Well spit it out, I don't have all day."

Judas pushed the piranha away from him, adjusting his tunic before taking the time to speak to Lucifer.

"Master, I want you to know I didn't do anything you think I have. Aziel possessed me for his own scheme. He's been working behind your back, Lord. He told me all about his plan, and he even tried to get me in on it!" Judas said, shooting me an evil grin of revenge.

Lucifer's cheeks went from black to red. His snarled, revealing sharp bloodied teeth, and violently spun his body around. He stared at Aziel and me with a look of pure evil.

"Aziel, is this true?" Lucifer asked.

Aziel looked at me and shook his head. He moved his lips, which allowed Lucifer to believe he was in the middle of an answer when I suddenly felt my body explode with a rush of euphoria. My eyes flashed white, and Aziel disappeared from in front of me. I tried to turn my head in order to search for him but found myself unable to.

As if I were watching a movie, I could only see what was happening around me and could not act upon it. Lucifer was screaming at the top of his lungs as the mob of piranhas ran at me. I watched myself fend off a dozen of them with agile moves I did not know my body was capable of.

Aziel had complete control over my body and was using it to defeat an army of piranha soldiers. Dozens of piranhas scattered the floor, as I watched my legs propel my body across the room.

"Get out of that body, Aziel!" Lucifer ordered from his throne.

I watched as Aziel lifted my hand up and flicked Lucifer the bird. I laughed subconsciously but stopped my laughter when I watched a piranha running at my body with a lethal spear in hand.

The piranha's teeth formed a cage of anger from which only spit escaped and dripped down his chin. He was getting closer by the moment, and I tried my hardest to jump out of the way or run out of danger. I could not budge a single muscle, and I could not understand why Aziel was forcing me to just stand there—did he want me to die?

"No you stupid fool! Don't do—" Lucifer screamed.

Before Lucifer could even finish his command, the piranha's spear had penetrated my heart. The sharp metal sliced cleanly through my flesh and punctured my heart. The spear exited the back of my body with a pop, and as the attacker yanked the weapon from my body, I fell to my knees and toppled over face first onto the floor.

A puddle of dark blood collected around my body and soaked my clothes and wetted my lips as they pressed against the ground. I could feel my body grow cold, and in my reflection on the marble floor, I could see my eyes fade to nothing.

25. Welcome to Paradise

Paradise is where everyone idealizes ending up after death. When speaking of Paradise, connotations of peace, harmony, and happiness first come to mind. Paradise is a place where shadows do not exist, a place where smiles are the nature of a face, a place where everyone should aspire to arrive.

Usually when a man becomes blind, the world is presented in darkness. However, I found myself blind, but the world was presented in a blinding light. I knew my eyes were wide open, but all I could see was brightness, as if I were staring onto a blank page.

Although I did not know where I stood, I did not feel lost. A hand placed itself on my shoulder, and I heard a whisper in my ear.

"Welcome home, Caleb."

"Who is that?" I immediately asked.

I felt two fingers press against my eyes and gently rub into them. Slowly the white faded into a blur of images and in time defined themselves.

The face I stared into was Aziel's, or at least the Aziel I had first met that I knew as Stranger. His dark brown hair was neatly parted, and his green eyes once again stared back at me strongly.

"Is that you, Aziel?" I asked.

Aziel smiled at me and walked away. I took the opportunity to look at my surroundings. I looked down and saw that I stood on clouds, which felt like cotton candy under my feet. The sky was a light blue, which was a hue away from white, and far off on the horizon stood a breathtaking golden gate. As I flashed back to my last moments in Hell, I quickly grabbed my chest, but found no wound was present.

I spun around quickly to look back at Aziel. He was brushing off his white robe, which extended to his knees. Aziel looked up at me and clapped his hands together.

"You did a beautiful job, Caleb."

"Uh, thank you? I'm sorry, Aziel, but I'm still very confused."

"Yes, I'm sorry about that. It was important for you not to know everything. Lucifer is very sly, and it had to appear real."

Aziel walked up and put his arm around me.

"Say, how furious do you think Lucifer is right now?"

We began to walk toward the golden gates, our feet cutting through the clouds like butter. Small specks of the clouds stuck between our toes like sand when you walk along a beach.

"So you didn't really sell me out or kill me?" I asked Aziel as we almost were reaching the gates.

"Well I didn't sell you out, at least not for real. We've got a lot planned for you, Caleb. You've just proven yourself worthy."

I did not know quite what to say. We now stood in front of the gate; a man was the only thing blocking me from Paradise. He wore a tunic similar to Aziel's and held a large book in his hand. Aziel took his arm off of me and shook hands with the man at the gate.

"Hello Pete, how's it going?" Aziel greeted.

Peter had curly brown hair and an expression of responsibility on his face. He turned to me and smiled. "What is your name?"

What is my name? My adventure, journey, test, or whatever you would like to call it, started with this very question. Yes, this was a question I had grown quite used to. The only difference now was that I knew the answer. I smiled at Aziel and answered Peter.

"My name is Caleb Stone."